Storm Warning

A bolt of lightning split the gray gloom and slashed through the trunk of a large tree on the bank behind the Vista Recreation bus.

Paige grabbed the metal divider behind the driver's seat. Startled by the explosive crack, Phoebe jumped forward. She reached for the divider to stop herself from sliding off the seat but touched the driver's shoulder instead.

The vision hit with all the power and fury of the storm, overwhelming Phoebe with raw panic.

A flash flood smashed into the bridge, collapsing the wooden framework. Caught in the middle of the structure when it buckled, the bus was battered by broken timbers and thrown against jagged rocks as it was swept away. . . .

Phoebe emerged from the premonition with one terrifying image lingering in her mind.

When the twisted remains of the bus finally settled to the bottom of the river, no one had escaped.

More titles in the

Pocket Books series

THE POWER OF THREE
KISS OF DARKNESS
THE CRIMSON SPELL
WHISPERS FROM THE PAST
VOODOO MOON
HAUNTED BY DESIRE
BEWARE WHAT YOU WISH
CHARMED AGAIN
SPIRIT OF THE WOLF

All Pocket Books are available by post from:
Simon & Schuster Cash Sales. PO Box 29
Douglas, Isle of Man IM99 1BQ
Credit cards accepted.
Please telephone 01624 836000
fax 01624 670923
Internet http://www.bookpost.co.uk
or email: bookshop@enterprise.net for details

SPIRIT OF THE WOLF

An original novel by Diana G. Gallagher

Based on the hit TV series created by

Constance M. Burge

POCKET
BOOKS

LONDON • SYDNEY • NEW YORK • TOKYO • SINGAPORE • TORONTO

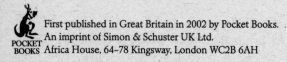
POCKET BOOKS First published in Great Britain in 2002 by Pocket Books.
An imprint of Simon & Schuster UK Ltd.
Africa House, 64–78 Kingsway, London WC2B 6AH

POCKET BOOKS and colophon are registered trademarks of Simon & Schuster.
A CIP catalogue record for this book is available from the British Library

ISBN 07434 30409

1 3 5 7 9 10 8 6 4 2

Printed by Cox and Wyman Ltd, Reading, Berkshire.

To Michael V. Price,
a dear friend of Abenaki descent,
with affection and gratitude for his
generous support and assistance

SPIRIT OF THE WOLF

Chapter

1

Phoebe Halliwell clutched a mug of steaming coffee in one hand and a plate with a banana and a warm cinnamon bun in the other. Elbowing the microwave oven door closed, she set her breakfast on the wooden table that dominated the kitchen of her homeand dropped into a chair. Starting today, she was going to double her efforts to find gainful employment.

Living on the brink of financial disaster is no fun, Phoebe thought as she clicked the Internet sign-on logo displayed on her laptop screen.

The Halliwell family wasn't broke, but maintaining the large Victorian house they had inherited from their grandmother was expensive. They weren't saving anything for emergencies, either— *not exactly a responsible fiscal policy for the world's first line of defense against an army of supernatural bad guys*, Phoebe thought wryly.

Still, Phoebe reminded herself, making the world safe for humanity was a labor of duty, not dollars. Shouldering that responsibility was the Charmed Ones' destiny, and they couldn't forsake it—not even when one of them had died trying to save an innocent.

Phoebe gave into a moment of grief for her oldest sister, Prue, who had been killed by the demon Shax while protecting a local doctor. Shaking off the sad thought, Phoebe brushed a wisp of hair behind her ear and clicked the e-mail icon. She still missed her sister terribly, but getting on with her life was the best way to honor Prue's memory.

"Earning my keep would certainly be a big step in that direction," Phoebe mumbled. Freeloading off her sisters made her uneasy, and she was determined to find a job. "Whether Piper likes it or not," she added.

Piper, the oldest Halliwell sister now that Prue was gone, owned and managed a popular nightclub called P3. Paige Matthews, their recently discovered younger half sister, had kept her job at the social services clinic when she'd moved into Halliwell Manor. Although Paige's salary combined with the profits from P3 barely covered the household expenses, Piper didn't want Phoebe to work. She believed that one of the Charmed Ones should be free to handle the never-ending supernatural crises they encountered on a moment's notice. Consequently, finding a job with flexible hours was an absolute necessity for Phoebe.

So far, that requirement had made it absolutely impossible to find anyone willing to hire her.

"And apparently things aren't looking up today, either." Phoebe sipped her coffee, her cheerful mood dimming as she scanned the list of new messages on the computer screen.

Five come-ons for get-rich-quick scams, three ads for cyber-store specials, and a reminder that her free trial subscription for an online lifestyle magazine was about to expire. Nothing from the job-search services she had recently signed up for, and no direct responses to her résumé listings.

Disgusted, Phoebe turned off the computer and pushed it aside. She was disappointed but not out of options. Since the marvels of modern technology weren't producing any results, she'd have to try job hunting the old-fashioned way, Phoebe decided with a flash of defiance. She pulled the classified section out of the morning newspaper, opened it to the Help Wanted ads, and picked up the cinnamon bun.

"Man, I am so late!" Paige paused inside the kitchen door to slip on low-heeled sandals. Her long dark hair was still slightly damp from the shower.

"At least you've got a job to be late for," Phoebe quipped.

"Yeah, but I'd rather not begin the day listening to Mr. Cowan yell, even if he is all bark and no bite." Paige's brown eyes focused on the cinnamon roll as Phoebe licked a dribble of gooey icing off her hand. "That looks good—and fattening."

Phoebe looked at Paige askance. "Fattening won't be a problem today because—"

"You're right," Paige interrupted. "I'm going to indulge now and skip lunch. You guys should have warned me that Piper was a great cook *before* I moved in."

Phoebe grinned as Paige lifted the top off the storage tin. The tall, younger woman didn't have to worry about ruining her willowy figure with a few hundred extra calories. Paige had a metabolism that burned potential fat faster than she could chew, but that wasn't what Phoebe had intended to point out.

"Sorry, Paige." Phoebe raised the cinnamon bun. "This is the last one."

"No fair!" Paige's full lips puckered into a playful pout.

"All's fair when it comes to grabbing Piper's last homemade cinnamon bun." Phoebe opened her mouth to take a bite. Her teeth clamped down on air filled with brilliant orb sparkles, and the cinnamon bun appeared in Paige's hand. "But using magic is so low."

"Oops!" Paige shrugged with a sheepish smile. "Guess I'm really hungry."

"So am I." Phoebe scowled, but she wasn't really angry. Half witch and half Whitelighter, Paige could orb things from one location to another with her mind. However, she hadn't learned to control the power yet and often moved objects without meaning to.

"Split it?" Paige tore the roll in half without waiting for an answer.

"Works for me." Phoebe held out her plate and turned her attention back to the newspaper. "I can't pound the pavement on an empty stomach."

"Any luck?" Paige poured a cup of coffee and leaned against the counter.

"Well, let's see." Phoebe's gaze quickly flicked up and down the columns of ads.

She had already applied for dozens of jobs in the bookkeeper, customer service, management trainee, and receptionist categories without any luck. They all required someone who could work nine to five, Monday through Friday, no excuses, no exceptions. Even the part-time night and weekend positions demanded people who would definitely be there nights and weekends, which pretty much eliminated most of her choices.

"Not unless I want to walk dogs, clean houses, or try to sell people stuff they don't want on the phone." Frustrated, Phoebe tossed the paper over her shoulder.

"You'd get plenty of exercise walking dogs." The corner of Paige's mouth twitched as she tried not to smile. "And the clients can't argue if they don't like the route of the day."

Knowing that Paige was trying to cheer her up, Phoebe cocked her head in mock consideration. "The exercise part is a good angle, and I could probably set my own hours—"

"You're not serious?" Paige's eyes widened.

"No way!" Phoebe laughed. "I'm getting desperate, but not desperate enough to consider a minimum wage job that includes close contact with fleas and doggie clean-up bags."

"Something will turn up soon." Paige raised her coffee cup to take another sip and glanced at her watch. "Think I should give Piper another wake-up call?"

"*Another* wake-up call?" Phoebe asked. Piper and her husband, Leo, had not had very much quality time together the past few weeks. When Leo wasn't off to dimensions unknown on pressing Whitelighter business, Piper was busy fighting a demon that wanted to kill someone or her or both. They had disappeared upstairs thirty seconds after Leo had orbed in late the night before. "Meaning that you've *already* disturbed them this morning?"

"Well, yeah," Paige said with an uncertain frown.

"You're lucky Piper didn't blow up the bedroom door!" Phoebe shuddered at the thought of a million high-speed splinters blasting the upstairs hallway. Piper's ability to freeze things by slowing the movement of molecules had expanded to include speeding them up. Before she had learned to control the new power, Piper had been stuck in demolition mode. Now her explosive accidents were rare, occurring only when she was extremely startled or upset.

Noting Paige's stricken expression, Phoebe softened her tone. "Why does Piper need a wake-up call?"

"She has to open P3 at nine for Security Plus," Paige explained. "It's eight-fifteen, which doesn't give her much time."

"Except that the installers will be there *tomorrow* at nine," Phoebe said. Piper had purchased a new security system for the club because thefts had increased in the area. The state-of-the-art Security Plus package came complete with a silent alarm that instantly alerted the police in the event of a break-in.

"Oh." Paige sighed. Piper had had more difficulty than Phoebe accepting Paige into the family and the Power of Three. Although they had all weathered the worst of the bumpy transition, little glitches such as disturbing Piper's sleep seemed more disastrous to Paige than they really were.

"And it's eight forty-five," Phoebe continued, "not eight-fifteen."

Paige looked at her watch again and sighed as she set her cup in the sink. "Guess I'm going to get yelled at after all. Better go."

The phone rang as Paige raced for the door.

Phoebe dashed for the phone and lifted the receiver with her fingers crossed. She had dozens of résumés out. With luck, her future boss was calling to set up an interview. "Hello. Phoebe Halliwell speaking."

"This is pathetic." Piper fluffed an old feather pillow, punched it with her fist, and coughed as dust billowed from the worn fabric. Waving the cloud away from the nest of old blankets, she settled back with a drawn-out sigh.

"Things could be worse." Leo slipped his arm around Piper and drew a faded patchwork quilt up to her chin.

"Yes, but since there obviously isn't an imminent demon disaster, nothing comes to mind," Piper grumbled. Roused from a deep sleep when Paige had pounded on the bedroom door, she and Leo had fled to the attic. Peace and quiet had become almost as rare around Halliwell Manor as privacy since the youngest sister witch had moved in.

"Pretend we're camping out," Leo suggested.

"I've never liked camping much." Piper dropped her head onto Leo's shoulder. Tired and worried about holding the Halliwell household together, she wasn't in a tolerant mood. "What's fun about sleeping on the cold, hard ground and being buzzed by bloodthirsty mosquitoes?"

"There aren't any mosquitoes up here." Leo glanced around the third-floor attic.

Piper pressed closer as she followed his gaze. The attic was a comfort in spite of the occasional evil invader, a haven filled with the ordinary and magical belongings collected by several Halliwell generations. Cast-off clothes, furniture, and sentimental treasures were piled along the walls. Only the area between the door and the pedestal that held *The Book of Shadows* was free of debris.

"Although there might be a bat or two napping in the rafters," Leo added.

"As long as there aren't any sisters," Piper said. "I'm grumpy when I haven't had enough sleep, and you know what *that* can do to my power controls."

Leo nodded solemnly. "Remind me to remind Paige while she's still in one piece."

Piper playfully punched Leo in the ribs, then stifled a yawn. They had stayed up late going over the P3 accounts looking for places to cut costs. She really couldn't afford a new security system right now, but she couldn't afford not to install one, either. They would suffer huge cash losses if the club had to close for repairs because it was robbed and vandalized.

"Uh-oh." Leo grabbed Piper's hands as the attic door flew open and Phoebe rushed in.

"What are you doing up here, Phoebe?" Piper asked as she wrenched free of Leo's hold.

Phoebe stopped abruptly. Her surprised gaze flicked from Piper to Leo and back again. "What are *you* two doing up here?"

"Trying to sleep without being interrupted." Piper's initial irritation quickly turned to concern. Phoebe didn't usually visit the attic unless she needed to consult *The Book of Shadows*. "Are we on monster alert?"

Phoebe shook her head. "No, I came up to find Prue's camera bag."

"Why?" Leo asked, tensing.

Piper knew that he was still worried about how she and Phoebe were coping with Prue's death. A combat medic who had died during World War II, he had the power to heal injured mortals. Although he couldn't magically erase the psychological wounds the Charmed witches sometimes suffered, his sensitive counsel was always welcome. However, Phoebe's quest didn't have anything to do with grief for their lost sister.

"Because I just accepted a paying job at *415*," Phoebe said.

"Really?" Piper blinked. Prue had done a lot of photographic work for the slick regional magazine. The assignments had been steady enough to provide a decent income while giving Prue the leeway to set her own schedule. For witch work purposes, a similar arrangement for Phoebe would be ideal. However, as far as Piper knew, Phoebe didn't have Prue's passion or talent for photography.

"A job or an assignment?" Leo asked with genuine interest.

"Assignment," Phoebe admitted. "But a small paycheck is better than no paycheck, right?" She began sorting through the pile of boxes that were filled with Prue's possessions.

"What's the assignment?" Leo wrapped his arms around his drawn-up knees.

"The editor needs a photographer to cover a pre-opening press weekend at a new resort in the mountains." Phoebe paused when she uncovered Prue's leather portfolio. Obviously shaken, she carefully set it aside. "It's a wilderness survival place for executives and other city types who want to pit themselves against the elements. Cool concept, huh?"

"You hate camping," Piper said.

"Not when it means making money," Phoebe countered.

"Good point," Piper agreed, "but why did Gil call you?"

"Prue told him she was going to ask me to go along as her assistant when she accepted this job months ago." Phoebe found the camera bag and placed it by the door. "I didn't bother to mention that her definition of an assistant was someone to help carry her equipment."

"But what if you don't get any usable photos?" Piper asked. "I'm not trying to discourage you, Phoebe, but you don't even know how to operate Prue's camera."

"There's a manual," Phoebe countered. "Besides, Prue once showed me how to use it. She wanted some updated shots of herself just in case the right guy popped into her life, so I volunteered to take them."

"How did they come out?" Piper raised an eyebrow.

"She loved a couple of them," Phoebe replied defensively, her eyes narrowing with determination. "I'm taking the assignment."

"You should," Leo agreed. "Prue probably thought it would be nice for the two of you to get away from it all for a few days."

"Yeah, that's what I thought, too," Phoebe said. "So since Vista Recreation is footing the bill, I thought I'd ask Paige if she wants to go. The freelance reporter 415 is sending to work with me will have a separate room."

Piper straightened suddenly. "If you and Paige are *both* gone, Leo and I will have the house to ourselves for a whole weekend."

"That fringe benefit did cross my mind." Phoebe winked at Leo. "So much has happened since you got married, you haven't had a honeymoon. I know spending a weekend home alone is—"

The image of a tall, dark, and very handsome man shimmered and solidified in the center of the room—Cole, Phoebe's boyfriend.

"—a poor substitute for a tropical cruise . . ." Phoebe's words trailed off with the unexpected intrusion.

"Okay!" Annoyed, Piper jumped up. She draped the tattered quilt over her shoulders and looked at the ceiling. "Who decided Leo and I couldn't sleep in this morning, and why?"

"I'm sure it's just a coincidence," Leo said with a hard glance at Cole.

"It feels like a cosmic conspiracy," Piper huffed.

Ignoring Piper and Leo, Cole focused on Phoebe. "You're going somewhere?"

"Sierra Sojourn, in the mountains next weekend." Phoebe looked away from her boyfriend as Piper swept toward the door, trailing the quilt like a regal train. "Where are you going, Piper?"

Leo shrugged as Piper threw open the door.

"Downstairs to cook something." Eyes flashing, Piper stomped into the hall. She was wide awake, hungry, and not at all sure she could control her temper or her super-speedy power. The last thing she wanted to do at the moment was clean up something she had blown to smithereens.

Phoebe flinched when the door slammed closed behind Leo. He quickly opened it again and stuck his head inside. "Sorry. I didn't mean to shove it that hard."

"No, I'm sorry, Leo," Phoebe said. "I didn't mean to upset Piper."

"Don't worry about it. She'll get over it, and I'll get pancakes." With an impish smile, Leo waved and closed the door again.

Phoebe relaxed when Cole placed his hands on her arms and turned her to face him. It didn't make sense to feel so safe in his presence, she thought as she met his intent gaze. Too many unknown factors could cause Belthazor, the muscular red demon that shared his existence, to emerge. Even though Belthazor hadn't tried to kill her or her sisters lately, she didn't trust Cole's worse half.

"What?" Phoebe asked, sensing that something was troubling him.

"Nothing, I just—" Cole hesitated, then released her. Placing one hand on his hip, he awkwardly shifted his weight and ran his other hand over his dark hair. "I, uh—don't think you should go off to the mountains for a weekend."

"I've taken a photography job Prue agreed to do months ago, Cole. It's work, not play." Phoebe raised her right hand. "I promise to have a completely miserable time."

"That's not what I'm worried about, Phoebe."

"Good," Phoebe said pointedly, "because Paige will probably go with me, and I don't want to spoil her fun."

"You're taking Paige?" Cole frowned, unable to hide that he really wasn't happy.

What is his problem, Phoebe wondered? Being half demon, Cole wasn't always Mr. Nice Guy, but he never acted like a jealous jerk. His attitude was unsettling, but she couldn't let it influence her decision.

"I haven't asked her, yet, but I don't think Paige will turn down a free vacation," Phoebe said. "She's young and adventurous, so she probably won't mind staying in a log cabin with no phone, no modem, no TV, and not a whole lot of other modern conveniences."

"You'll be completely cut off from everything and everyone?" Cole asked. "Even Piper and Leo?"

"Yeah," Phoebe drawled. "One of the perks is that Leo and Piper will have three days home alone. You're the only one who seems to have a problem with it."

"Because it's not safe," Cole said.

Phoebe struggled to keep her mounting irritation in check. Arguing with Cole wouldn't put his irrational reservations to rest. She tried basic facts. "Sierra Sojourn is staffed with professionals who have lots of experience surviving in the woods. It's just a glorified camping trip."

"Maybe it is, and maybe it isn't." Cole leaned forward slightly to punctuate his next remark. "What if *they*"—he glanced up—"are positioning you and Paige to protect an innocent?"

Startled, Phoebe blinked. That possibility hadn't occurred to her, but it didn't seem likely. Gil had had a perfectly logical reason for asking her to take Prue's place on the press junket.

The leather portfolio Phoebe had leaned against a stack of boxes suddenly slid to the floor. Cole jumped with a sharp intake of breath.

He whirled to confront the blank wall, his fist drawn back to unleash an energy ball.

"Is something after you?" Phoebe asked, then winced. It was a foolish question.

These days something sinister was always trying to track down Cole. He had been on the run since his love for her had enabled him to conquer the evil part of his nature. As punishment, the Source had put a price on his head. No sooner had Cole vanquished one bounty hunter than another, more ruthless mercenary took its place.

"Let me rephrase that," Phoebe continued. "Is a *specific* something after you?"

"I'm not sure." Still tense, Cole wandered toward the window. He hugged the wall as he scanned the yard below. "The word on the street is that Q'hal swore a blood oath to hunt me down. He won't give up until I'm dead—or he is."

"Is Q'hal more dangerous than the usual demonic creeps that have tried to kill you?" Phoebe asked.

"Nothing I can't handle," Cole assured her with a smile. "I just don't want *you* to get in the line of fire. Q'hal doesn't care who gets hurt as long as he gets his man—or demon."

Ordinarily, Phoebe wouldn't let a little danger come between her and the love of her life. This time, however, Cole's concern for her safety worked to her advantage.

"So I'll be safer in the mountains," Phoebe said. "Until you defeat Q'hal, anyway."

"Now that you mention it, that's probably true." Cole held out his arms and drew Phoebe into his embrace. He touched his lips to her hair and spoke softly. "Although I'm not sure I can stand being away from you for three days."

"Don't even think about shimmering into the mountains to visit!" Phoebe pushed away, her tone and expression stern. "Sierra Sojourn is three hours away from the nearest town. If somebody up there saw you, there's no way I could explain how you managed to just drop in."

"Point taken." Cole pulled her back against his chest. "I'll still worry about you, though."

"I'll be fine," Phoebe insisted. "I can use a relaxing weekend away from the city and my Charmed responsibilities."

Provided that Cole's theory was wrong, Phoebe mused. Nothing in her life was predictable, so it was entirely possible that she and Paige *were* being sent to Sierra Sojourn to save an innocent from some unknown evil.

If so, they probably wouldn't know whom they had to save from what until they got there.

Chapter

2

Although Phoebe's bedroom door was ajar and the light was on, Paige hesitated before knocking. Her wrong-day wake-up call on Monday morning had prompted a series of lectures from Phoebe, Piper, and Leo. They had all made it quite clear that, since the Charmed Ones often had to drop everything to rescue someone at any hour of the day or night, uninterrupted z's were a precious commodity.

Paige sighed. Her present problem didn't meet the no-other-recourse emergency standard Piper had set, but she needed an answer. "Which I can't get unless I ask the question," Paige muttered as she peeked through the narrow crack between the door and the doorjamb. Phoebe was sitting cross-legged on her bed.

"Is someone there?" Phoebe stopped writing in a spiral-bound notebook and looked up.

"It's just me." Paige opened the door a little more and raised her hand in a tentative wave. "Are you busy?"

"Yeah, but not so busy that I don't have time to talk to a sister." Phoebe dropped her pen and clasped her hands in her lap. "What's up?"

Paige's apprehensions melted away under the warmth of Phoebe's smile. She couldn't help but wonder if she'd ever be totally comfortable with the sibling squabbles that Piper and Phoebe took in stride. Not only was she the new kid in the Halliwell house, she had been raised as an only child. Adapting to a family dynamic was harder than she had imagined.

"I was just getting my stuff ready to go tomorrow, and I wasn't sure if I should pack my hair dryer." Paige perched on the edge of the bed.

"Why not?" Phoebe sat back slightly, perplexed.

"Because you said there was no TV and no phones or modems," Paige explained. "There's no point bringing a hair dryer if there's no electricity."

"Good point. Not a problem." Phoebe picked up a color brochure and flipped through the pages. "There isn't any phone service because Sierra Sojourn is too remote for regular phone lines, and it's out of cell phone range. However, according to this—"

Paige took the brochure Phoebe held out. It was folded open to a picture of a large building with log siding and a wide veranda that ran the length of one side. The sand- and gray-colored stonework of a massive fireplace filled a third of the end wall and tapered into a squat chimney. The chimney was dwarfed by an array of dark, rectangular panels that covered the roof.

"That's the community building and mess hall," Phoebe said, "also known as the Lodge. It gets electrical power from an 'environmentally friendly solar panel collection and battery storage system.' I can't wait to get more info on that."

"Sounds kind of high-tech for a rustic retreat," Paige observed, handing the brochure back.

"The ultimate in alternative energy technology but limited to the main building." Phoebe tucked the brochure into a file folder on her nightstand. "The cabins don't have electricity yet, so we'll have to go to the community building for hot showers, indoor plumbing, and meals."

"Oh." Paige had been so delighted when Phoebe invited her to go that she hadn't asked about conditions at the mountain resort. Until now, her idea of roughing it had been a picnic in the park, but she wasn't too concerned about fitting in. Anyone who could adapt to being a witch without warning could handle a few days of pioneer living.

"At least we'll be getting hot meals," Phoebe

added, teasing. "When Sierra Sojourn is offi-
cially open for business, anyone who signs up
for the deluxe package has to build a shelter and
forage for food. Except for emergencies, they
won't have *any* access to the camp compound—
rain or shine."

"And how much will people pay for that
privilege?" Paige asked.

"Let me put it this way," Phoebe said. "I'd
have to win the lottery to afford it."

Paige sighed. So many of her clinic's clients
could barely afford to house and feed their families. It seemed like a cruel joke that rich people
would spend small fortunes to freeze and go
hungry on a wilderness survival vacation.

"I think I'll leave the hair dryer behind."
Paige noticed Phoebe's camper backpack on the
floor. The canvas bag was larger than the discount store variety but smaller than Paige's duffel. It was also only half full. "You haven't
finished packing, either, huh?"

"No, I'm done." Phoebe leaned over to look
into the backpack. "Except for my bathroom
stuff, a warm jacket, and my notebook. All the
photography equipment fits in the camera bag.
I'll be wearing my jeans and boots."

Paige nodded, wondering if she should travel
a little lighter than she had planned. In addition
to one pair of jeans and her hiking boots, Phoebe
was taking only the barest essentials: socks,
underwear, a few long- and short-sleeved T-

shirts, a paperback novel, and a flashlight.

"I should probably bring a flashlight, too," Paige said.

"You'll need one if you want to read in bed after dark." Phoebe picked up her pen and glanced at the spiral-bound notebook lying open on the bed. "Or work on your notes."

"Notes on what?" Paige asked.

"Vista Recreation, Incorporated." Phoebe pulled the file folder off the nightstand. It was full of press clippings. "I've been doing some background research."

"I thought the magazine was sending someone else to handle the reporting," Paige said. "Agnes or Anna?"

"Angie Swanson. Gil said she'd meet us in Lone Pine River." Phoebe closed the notebook, dropped the file on top of it, and leaned back against her pillow. "We'll be hooking up with all the other journalists at Hawk's Café and General Store."

Paige dropped onto her side and propped her head in her hand. "What if Angie gets upset because you're taking over her job?"

"She won't," Phoebe said.

"How can you be so sure?" Paige didn't know any reporters, but she was acquainted with a few artists and musicians. They were all highly competitive, and none of them would let an amateur muscle into their territory without a fight.

"For one thing, Angie isn't an investigative

reporter. She specializes in physical fitness and
writes an occasional article about unusual vaca-
tions. I haven't met her yet because she was
pushing to meet a deadline." Phoebe arched an
eyebrow to emphasize her punch line. "For a
piece about local celebrity workouts and diets."

Paige frowned, confused. "Doesn't Sierra
Sojourn qualify as an unusual vacation spot?"

"Yes, but it isn't Vista Recreation's *first*
wilderness resort project." Phoebe narrowed her
dark eyes as she leaned forward. "The corporate
plan is to develop, own, and operate outdoor
theme resorts across the country."

"Uh-huh." Paige nodded, but she didn't
understand what exactly was bothering Phoebe
about Vista Recreation. There wasn't anything
odd about a corporation that wanted to expand.
"Why is that a problem?"

"Maybe it isn't." Phoebe leaned back with her
hands behind her head. Her intent gaze focused
on empty space. "I don't know yet."

"But you think something fishy might be
going on," Paige said.

"The company's first project, Tropical Trek,
opened in central Florida two years ago,"
Phoebe explained, "but not without some legal
complications."

"Legal or evil?" Paige asked.

"Both definitions might be appropriate,"
Phoebe said. "Several area residents claimed
that they were forced to sell their property to

Vista Recreation at below-market prices. When some refused, the lands were condemned, so they had no choice but to take the corporation's paltry offers."

"That's a major bad." Paige's outrage mounted as she listened.

"Yeah." Phoebe continued. "The residents sued, but they couldn't prove that the local authorities were working in collusion with the corporation. Tropical Trek's presence turned their miserable, bug-infested backwater into a boomtown, and several local bigwigs cashed in. The residents who were cheated lost the case."

"Figures." Paige sighed, disgusted and dismayed. The odds rarely favored ordinary people who took wealthy corporations to court. It was hard to compete against legal departments with mega-bucks and resources. "Is the same kind of rip-off going on at Sierra Sojourn?"

Phoebe shook her head. "No, but the land was under federal government control—until Vista Recreation acquired the rights to develop it."

"Somebody may have pulled some influential strings, but that's not necessarily illegal," Paige said.

"Agreed." Phoebe shrugged. "The evil in this situation seems to be simple human greed and not anything supernatural."

"When did something supernatural get factored into the equation?" Paige asked with a start.

"Supernatural is always part of the equation." Smiling, Phoebe patted Paige's arm. "Fate has this nasty habit of making sure that one of us is on the scene whenever an innocent is in trouble."

"Right." Paige raised her hands as though to cement that fact in her mind. "I keep forgetting how that works."

"Don't worry," Phoebe said. "All the ins and outs of the whole magical thing will become second nature in no time."

"In the meantime, I could use an official Charmed Ones handbook," Paige quipped.

Maude Billie hung a long-handled ladle on the rack suspended above the central prep station, completing the collection of spatulas, spoons, and tongs. Then, folding flabby arms over an ample chest, she stepped back to survey the spacious kitchen.

Unlike the basic frontier décor in the rest of the Lodge, the Sierra Sojourn kitchen was completely modern. Light from multiple ceiling fixtures reflected off stainless-steel work surfaces and cabinets. Built-in ovens and stoves, the industrial dishwasher, and a large walk-in cooler with attached freezer were all energy efficient and positioned for easy access.

No more aching back because she had to bend over to baste a turkey, Maude thought. She rubbed her aching hip, reluctant to acknowledge the first signs of arthritis. During thirty-two years as a professional cook, she had flipped burgers with short-order tyrants in neighborhood diners and created gourmet delicacies for arrogant chefs in exclusive country clubs. Now she was finally the boss chef in the kitchen of her dreams. It would take a lot more than a few aches and pains to get her to retire now.

Something white flashed past the small window in the back door, catching Maude's eye. She blinked and refocused, but all she saw was darkness beyond the glass.

"Is there anything else you want done tonight, Maude?" Sonja Larson shoved a large pot into a lower cabinet.

Startled, Maude stared at the young woman for a long moment. Twenty-five, soft-spoken, and petite with short, blond hair and blue eyes, Sonja was the dining room supervisor and Maude's exact opposite. They got along great.

"What's the hurry?" Maude asked.

"Kyle rented a couple of new videos," Sonja explained. "Kind of a last fling for everyone since we won't be able to use the TV after the press party gets here tomorrow."

Maude nodded, even though she didn't share the sense of loss. Eventually, the resort would be equipped with a satellite system for television reception. Until then, the TV functioned solely as a monitor for the VCR. Although the supervisory staff had been free to use the resort's facilities during the setup phase, leisure time activities would be restricted once paying guests were on the premises.

"Kyle has already staked out one of the couches," Sonja said.

"I bet," Maude said. Fifty-four, with a brusque manner and burly build, she had never married and never regretted it. She had *always* been too set in her ways to cater to a man. Sonja, on the other hand, adored her husband, Kyle, the assistant chef and baker. Thirty-two, with boyish good looks and a perpetual grin, Kyle idolized Sonja, too.

"Exactly!" Sonja laughed. "Carlos said Ben can return the movies to the video store when he drives the reporters back to town on Sunday. We watch them tonight or not at all—at least not on this six bucks." She cocked her head with a questioning expression, waiting for an answer.

"Go on. Get out of here." Maude rolled her eyes, feigning exasperation. Sonja and Kyle had worked hard the past two weeks, helping her get the kitchen operational. They deserved a break. "We can finish in the morning."

"Thanks, Maude. You're a doll." Sonja tossed her apron in the laundry basket and paused before she pushed through the swinging doors into the mess hall. "Just about everyone is getting together tonight. Don't you want to come?"

"No, I'll pass." Maude absently smoothed the graying brown hair she wore in a tight bun. The severe, sanitary style suited her occupation and disposition.

"Okay, but you'll be sorry you missed *Space Race 2500*," Sonja teased on her way out.

"I don't think so," Maude muttered. She locked the double swinging door behind Sonja and glanced out the wide pass-through in the wall.

Doris Cirelli, the thin, thirty-something head housekeeper and resident nurse, dashed into the mess hall from the wing that formed an L off the kitchen. A stickler for rules and details, Doris was responsible for the infirmary, community lavatories, and laundry and didn't interfere in kitchen business. For Maude, that was the ideal working relationship.

"Have you seen the girls?" Doris asked Sonja, referring to Jan and Dona Mueller. The twin sisters were working their way through college and had signed on as housekeeping crew for the summer.

Nobody had been able to satisfactorily explain to Maude why rich people who wanted to learn wilderness survival skills couldn't make their own beds.

"Over there." Sonja pointed to the furniture arranged in front of the TV at the far end of the large, rectangular room.

Doris pushed her wire-rimmed glasses back onto her narrow nose and hurried over to join them.

Both young women wore their long dark hair

in ponytails perched high on their heads. They were curled up on a large, overstuffed sofa watching Harley Smith set logs into the huge stone fireplace.

"Light that fire, Harley," Jan said.

"It's lit." Attractive in a lean, middle-aged, weather-beaten way, with a military-style buzz cut, Harley was one of several wilderness encounter experts Vista Recreation had hired. The job was to make sure the customers went home unharmed and feeling that they had met and mastered the hazards of an unforgiving mountainous environment.

"Feels good." Dona pulled a fleece throw over her legs.

Even in summer, a blazing fire was needed to take the chill off the night air. All the staff and guest cabins had been equipped with wood-burning stoves, a concession to comfort that Maude found particularly pleasing.

"Somebody else can bring in more wood." Harley stood up and stretched with a grunt.

"I will." Kyle sprang to his feet. His affable grin widened when Sonja walked up.

Maude pulled the folding shutters closed over the pass-through as he planted a kiss on his wife's cheek. Although she appreciated the crew's good-natured civility, she could only take so much cozy camaraderie. She'd much rather spend her downtime under a warm comforter with a paperback thriller.

After grabbing a large flashlight hanging by the back door, Maude slipped on her sweater and turned out the lights. The sense of security she felt in the kitchen vanished the instant she stepped outside. A shiver of apprehension tingled her spine as she locked the door.

"Get a grip," Maude muttered, convinced that her mind had been playing tricks the past few nights. There had to be a logical explanation for the wisps of white she had seen flitting through the moonlit forest. She did not believe in ghosts.

Training the flashlight beam on the dirt path, Maude headed toward the cluster of employee cabins that everyone except Doris called home. The nurse had a room off the infirmary so she would be instantly available. In a serious medical emergency, help could be summoned on the radio in the office across the hall. Three rooms at the far end of the wing were reserved for visiting Vista Recreation VIPs. Most of the employees bunked two to a cabin. Maude Billie and Carlos Martinez, the general manager, each had a cabin to themselves.

A rustling noise in the darkness ahead brought Maude up short. She tightened her grip on the flashlight and then relaxed when Carlos stepped into the light.

"Evenin', Maude." Carlos nodded and touched the brim of his Australian bush hat. A rifle rested casually in the crook of his other arm.

A small, wiry man with curly black hair, he seldom smiled. "All locked up for the night?"

"I locked the back door and the doors into the mess hall," Maude said. "Everyone is still in the Lodge, watching a movie. They just started the tape, so you haven't missed much."

"I've got better ways to spend my time," Carlos said.

Guard duty, Maude guessed. Carlos was as serious about his job as she was about hers. An expert woodsman with a national reputation and a master's degree in business administration, he was as proficient in the wild as he was in the manager's office. It was no secret, though, that he'd rather be tracking a deer than sitting at a desk. She was sure he enjoyed patrolling the grounds.

"Find anything?" Maude asked with a glance at the rifle.

A series of harmless but annoying pranks had plagued the resort since construction had begun. William DeLancey, the founder and CEO of Vista Recreation, blamed a local Native American tribe and wanted the culprits caught before Sierra Sojourn opened.

"No, it's pretty quiet," Carlos said as he moved on. "Take care, Maude."

"I will." Maude breathed deeply as Carlos turned down the trail toward the guest cabins. Between the pranks and the eerie white wisps, she was more nervous than she wanted to

admit—to herself or anyone else, especially
Carlos. He was only barely tolerant of those he
perceived as weak.

An owl hooted, heightening the tension that
seemed to hover over the forest. From the corner
of her eye, Maude saw a sliver of smoke snake
through the trees. Anxious to reach the safety of
her cabin, she broke into a lumbering jog.

Her feet thudded on a natural cushion of pine
needles and leaves as she ran past darkened cabins. Her breathing was labored when she
reached the base of the two-tiered steps onto her
front stoop. As she started to climb, a large tree
standing off the cabin's front corner burst into
flames.

Maude stumbled backward a step, stunned as
the air around her was vacuumed into the vora-
cious inferno. She gawked for a long moment,
unable to comprehend the sudden, inexplicable
event. Then she latched onto the first thought
that entered her mind: She had to save her stuff!

Although most of her things were in storage,
Maude had brought a few, more precious possessions to the resort. Having her mother's
framed photo, her hand-embroidered throw pillows, several favorite books, and other trinkets
scattered around had changed the impersonal,
rustic room into a homey haven. She couldn't let
her treasures burn.

Ignoring the heat, Maude sprang onto the
porch and threw open the cabin door. A strange

thumping noise was barely audible in the roar of the intense fire outside. Heart pounding, she raised her flashlight as she moved inside.

The wooden bed frame on the far wall was rising and falling repetitively, beating an uneven cadence on the floor. One of the throw pillows bounced to the edge of the mattress and fell off. Everything else in the room was still stationary.

Instinct told Maude to flee. Instead she froze, her gaze fastened on the snarling face of the gray wolf filling the doorway, blocking her escape.

Carlos leaned against a large boulder near the last cabin on the camp's perimeter. A hundred miles of dense virgin forest separated Vista Corporation's newest enterprise from the small town of Lone Pine River. The isolated resort was insignificant compared with the primal grandeur of the mountain it invaded. It was his job to protect it—from financial failure and from all external threats.

On guard, Carlos had all his senses tuned to the dark surroundings. His nostrils flared with the tang of pine and the musty scent of rotting leaves and damp moss. Barely discernible shadows moved through a darkness broken only by the flicker of stars. The crack of snapping twigs as something crashed through the brush brought him to instant attention.

"Carlos?" Maude called in a hoarse whisper.

"Over here, Maude." Carlos turned on his

flashlight and aimed the light to intersect the frantic woman's shaking beam.

"Thanks goodness I found you." Maude clutched her stomach, gasping. Her clothes were covered with dirt, and leaves clung to her hair. Blood from a gash on her knee stained her torn white cotton pants.

"What happened?" Carlos rushed to Maude's side. His first inclination was to blame the vandals who had been sabotaging the resort the past year. The incidents had ranged from stolen machinery parts to axle-busting potholes on the dirt access road or spooky light displays in the woods. All the pranks had been engineered to waste time and money and play on the nerves. No one had been seriously hurt.

"Have to—catch—my breath." Speaking between gulps for air, Maude stumbled to a nearby log and sat down. "I went into the cabin to save my mother's picture because the tree suddenly caught on fire, but the bed was jumping up and down, so I couldn't, and then the wolf came to the door."

"You were running from a wolf?" Carlos clipped the flashlight onto his belt, leaving his hands free to shoot. A renegade wolf was a problem he didn't need just as a busload of press was due to arrive.

"No." Maude shook her head. "It ran away from me and—and then it disappeared—into thin air. Gone." She snapped her fingers. "Just like that."

Maude was babbling, but she wasn't prone to hysterics. Since burning trees and shaking beds could be rigged, Carlos didn't dismiss her story. The wolf was more worrisome because human intervention couldn't explain its behavior. Only a sick or injured animal that was driven by hunger or crazed by pain would venture so close to a cabin. *The wolf was dangerous*, Carlos thought, *and Maude is lucky to be alive*.

"Come on." Carlos cupped Maude's elbow and urged her to her feet. "I'll walk you over to the Lodge, and then I'll check out your cabin."

"Oh, no. I'm going with you." Maude pulled a dry leaf off her sweater and squared her shoulders.

"Not a good idea," Carlos said firmly. If the wolf attacked, he didn't want to be distracted by worrying about her safety. "If someone is still hanging around—"

Maude cut him off. "I didn't run to the Lodge in the first place because I didn't want to panic anyone, especially with all those reporters coming tomorrow. I'm sure Mr. DeLancey's idea of advance publicity doesn't include headlines about haunted forests, human-hunting wolves, or trees that spontaneously combust."

"Of course not," Carlos conceded, "but stuff like this doesn't happen for no reason."

"I totally agree," Maude said, nodding. "But if some of those Sinoyat people tried to scare me tonight because they're still trying to run Vista

Corporation off this mountain, I don't think Mr. DeLancey wants to advertise *that*, either."

Carlos sighed. She had a good point, and he didn't have a good counterargument. John Hawk, the elderly chief of the Sinoyat, was committed to shutting down Sierra Sojourn because it had been built on "stolen tribal lands," or so he claimed. The Native American tribe hadn't taken the matter to court because they couldn't prove their claim. Instead, they had resorted to delay and scare tactics. At least, that's what he and Mr. DeLancey believed.

Now, if Maude wasn't exaggerating, Carlos thought as they headed back toward the staff cabins, the tricks had suddenly escalated from inconvenient and unpleasant to dangerous and destructive.

"Which tree?" Carlos asked when they reached Maude's cabin. He hadn't seen or heard anything unusual on the short hike from the guest quarters.

"That one." Maude trained her flashlight on a large pine just off the front corner of the small building.

"You sure?" Carlos walked over to examine the rough bark. The trunk wasn't hot or charred, and the needles on the lower branches were still green.

"Positive," Maude insisted. "The whole thing was in flames. I *know* I didn't imagine it."

"Must have been some kind of illusion, then,"

Carlos said. "One of those holographic projection things." He didn't actually believe that, but he didn't want Maude to come unhinged. Her assistant, Kyle Larson, was primarily a baker, and it was too late to import another cook for the press weekend.

"I suppose that's possible." Frowning, Maude followed Carlos inside. She turned on both battery-powered lamps while he checked the bed.

There was no evidence of wires or anything else that the wooden bed frame had been rigged to bounce.

"Anything?" Maude asked. She opened the front of the woodstove and stuffed bits of kindling into the firebox.

"Nothing I can see, but I wouldn't rule out a small, localized earth tremor." Carlos pushed his hat back and scratched his forehead.

"A quake that only affected the bed?" Maude struck a match and lit the dry tinder. She glanced back with skeptical eyes, then tossed a couple of logs into the stove.

"Not likely, but not impossible," Carlos admitted. "The ground under that particular wall could be less stable."

"Well, I like that theory better than blaming it on ghosts." Dusting her hands off, Maude closed the stove and turned. "Not that I've seen any. Ghosts, I mean."

"Phosphor sheens," Carlos said. He clarified in response to Maude's puzzled expression.

"Mosses, lichen—things that naturally glow in the dark. Like fireflies."

"Moss?" Maude laughed, a little too loudly, Carlos noticed. She was unnerved but not freaking out. "So the swooping motions are just optical illusions?"

"Or ghosts," Carlos deadpanned.

"I'll believe that when you do," Maude shot back.

Satisfied that the cabin was safe, Carlos turned toward the door. "I'll be patrolling between here and the Lodge until everyone's tucked in tonight. Just as a precaution. Holler if you need anything."

Carlos waited until Maude bolted the door before he flicked on his flashlight. He spent several minutes scanning the ground around the tree and cabin. He didn't know how the tricksters had convinced Maude she had seen things that weren't there, but he was certain the Sinoyat were guilty. Maybe someone had broken into the kitchen and spiked her container of herbal tea with a native hallucinogen. Nothing would surprise him, including that they hadn't left even a footprint.

The wolf was another matter.

Carlos didn't know if Maude had really seen a wolf or not. Either way, he had to act cautiously and assume that a rogue was stalking the camp. Invigorated by the prospect of the hunt, Carlos darted through the woods with only one thought in mind: The safety of the staff and guests was more important than protecting an endangered species that had become a menace. When he found the beast, he would have to kill it.

Needing more ammunition, Carlos opened the door of his cabin and carefully moved across the room in the dark. His heart lurched when he turned on the lamp by the bed.

Resting on his pillow was the bleached skull of a wolf.

Blood oozed from the empty eye sockets.

Chapter

3

"There it is." Phoebe pointed out the windshield of Paige's VW Beetle. The interior was cramped, but driving the economical car into the mountains had saved a bundle in gas.

"I hope the coffee's fresh." Paige activated the turn signal, down shifted, and steered the lime green Bug across the opposite lane and into the restaurant driveway.

The Mountain High Café shared a large dirt and gravel parking lot with Hawk's General Store and Gas. Situated on the outskirts of the small town of Lone Pine River, both businesses occupied rambling one-story buildings with weathered wood siding and neon signs in the windows. They were the first evidence of civilization Phoebe and Paige had seen since they had turned off the interstate an hour earlier.

Phoebe checked the instruction sheet the

magazine had provided and waved toward the
far side of the café, where several cars were
already lined up. "We're supposed to park over
there."

To preserve the wilderness ambience of Sierra
Sojourn, employees and guests would be trans-
ported to the site by a bus, which apparently
hadn't arrived yet. Vista Recreation paid the café
for parking privileges. As a bonus, the café
would get a stream of customers who wanted to
eat and drink before or after the three-hour drive
to and from the mountain resort.

Paige whipped the car into a space, pulled on
the emergency brake, and shut down the engine.
"Okay, we're here. Now what do we do?"

"Eat." Phoebe folded the directions and
stuffed the paper in a side pocket on the camera
bag. Fortified with Piper's apple coffee cake and
bottles of chilled juice, they had hit the road at
dawn. Neither she nor Paige had been hungry
when they had stopped to top off the gas tank a
couple of hours ago. She hoped they had time
for lunch before the bus left.

"And find Angie Swanson," Phoebe added.
The photos for the 415 article were her first pri-
ority, and she was anxious to make a good first
impression on her freelance partner.

"What did Gil say she looked like again?"
Paige pocketed her keys and glanced out the
back window.

"Verbatim?" Phoebe cocked her head and

recited the editor's description of Angie word for word. "'Too tall, too thin, with too much shocking red hair, and pretty—if you like freckles.'"

"Then we've found Angie," Paige said.

Phoebe craned her neck to look. A willowy woman with a cascading mane of curly red hair was striding across the parking lot, pulling a wheeled suitcase. Wearing snug designer jeans, a braided leather belt, heeled boots, and a stylish sea green blouse, she was a walking advertisement for expensive and completely inappropriate outdoor fashion.

"Who's that?" Paige asked.

Phoebe followed her sister's gaze down the line of parked cars to the obvious object of interest—a man with a mop of sandy blond hair and a classically handsome profile. Of average height and build, he wore bleached-out jeans, scuffed boots, and a blue blazer over a Western-style white shirt.

"Don't know," Phoebe said as the man slammed the back of an SUV closed. Compared with Cole's dark and dangerous, cosmopolitan sex appeal, the stranger's clean-cut good looks were kind of bland. Still, she could see why he had attracted Paige's attention. "He is cute, huh?"

"If you like older, ruggedly handsome guys in cowboy clothes," Paige said with a huff of disdain.

"He can't be more than thirty-five." Phoebe glanced toward the man again, wondering why he looked familiar.

"Like I said—older." Paige flipped down the windshield visor to check her reflection in a small, built-in mirror.

Curious, Phoebe watched as the man headed across the parking lot with his head bent over a magazine. She rolled down the car window but not quickly enough to stop him from colliding with Angie.

Flustered, the man stepped back. "I am *so* sorry. Are you okay?"

"I'm fine." Angie glowered at the man for a moment before a look of recognition crossed her face. Her frown was instantly replaced by a dazzling smile. "Mitch Rawlings, isn't it? I'm Angie Swanson with *415*."

Phoebe grabbed Paige's arm and whispered, "That's Mitch Rawlings!"

Paige fixed her with a blank expression. "Who?"

"He writes for *National Weekly*," Phoebe explained. "We're talking some top-notch journalistic company here."

Mitch Rawlings was an investigative reporter who wrote about political corruption for the slick news magazine. In the past year he had uncovered a dishonest federal judge, cleared a Congressman accused of campaign finance infractions, and foiled a corporate plot to illegally acquire water rights in a drought-ridden Western state. The guy had credentials to burn.

"That's nice." Completely not impressed, Paige pushed open the car door. "I've got to work the kinks out of my legs. Coming?"

Nodding, Phoebe stepped out of the car and grabbed the camera bag. She handed a box of film and a twenty-dollar bill to Paige. "As long as you're going for a walk, anyway, would you mind getting me six more rolls at that store over there?"

"Sure." Taking the film and money, Paige eyed the bulging side of the camera bag. "Twelve rolls aren't enough?"

"The more pictures I take, the better my chances of getting a few shots the magazine can actually use. Wait—" Phoebe fished another twenty out of the bag, which was doubling as a purse. "Get me three disposable cameras, too. Just in case something goes wrong with the fancy one."

"Better safe than sorry." Paige frowned. "Maybe I should get some more lollipops."

"My treat." Phoebe inhaled and exhaled slowly. "Now, here's hoping that I can pass myself off as a professional photographer."

As Paige headed for the general store, Phoebe walked toward the two reporters, who were still talking in the middle of the parking lot.

"—for me, it's a paid vacation," Mitch was saying.

"I had no idea you were an accomplished outdoors person, Mr. Rawlings." Angie did not acknowledge Phoebe with a word or a glance as she approached.

Just rude, Phoebe wondered, *or too starstruck by the famous Mr. Rawlings to notice anyone else?*

"Call me Mitch." Sensing someone coming up behind him, Mitch turned and smiled at Phoebe. "Hi, there. Are you part of the Sierra Sojourn group?"

"Yes, I am. Phoebe Halliwell, photographer for *415.*"

"Then you must know Angie," Mitch said.

"Yes, we're partners on this assignment, although we haven't actually met yet." Phoebe held out her hand. "Hi, Angie. I'm looking forward to working with you this weekend."

"Yeah, me, too." Angie's wan smile and limp handshake left no doubt she didn't appreciate the intrusion. "Listen, Phoebe. We can get together to talk about the article later, okay? Mitch and I were just going inside for a quick bite."

"We've got some time to kill before the bus gets here." Mitch folded his magazine and slipped it into his jacket pocket. "It's going to be a long ride. Why don't you join us, Phoebe?"

"I'd love to," Phoebe said, pleased by the instant acceptance from the renowned reporter. Angie wasn't nearly as welcoming. In fact, Phoebe thought with a glance at her partner, *if looks were flaming daggers, I'd be charred shish-kebob.*

"What time is it?" Shielding her eyes from the light, Piper stretched under the sheets.

Leo stepped back from the closet to look at the clock on the nightstand. "Twelve-fifteen."

"Twelve? Noon?" Piper hugged her pillow and grinned. "I feel downright decadent."

"And rested, too, I'll bet." Pulling on a shirt, Leo moved to the chest of drawers. "You've been asleep for ten hours."

"A double dose of shut-eye," Piper teased. Although she often worked late at P3, she didn't usually have the luxury of sleeping in as long as she wanted.

Most mornings her sisters were thumping around banging doors, running showers, and yakking while they got ready to go to or look for work. Today the house had been totally void of noise and interruptions because Paige and Phoebe were gone. No ill-mannered, murderous demons had dropped in unannounced, either. The weekend was off to a great start.

Throwing off the covers, Piper slipped into the satin robe she had tossed aside the night before. "Are you hungry?"

"I could eat." Leo bent over to look under the bed for his shoes.

"Me, too." Piper's stomach rumbled. "Think I'll go down and fire up the stove."

The phone rang before Piper reached the door. Leo answered. "Inspector Morris. What's up?"

Halting in the doorway, Piper gave into a moment of wishful thinking. Maybe the police inspector had called to ask for a donation to some cop charity. *Not likely*, she thought with a sigh. Darryl Morris knew that Piper and her sisters were witches. Whenever something weird went down on the local crime scene, he called for help, advice, or both.

"Isn't that *your* job?" Leo threw Piper a helpless look.

Piper glared back. They had been saving discount coupons for the local video store for weeks. The day before, Leo had used them at the Movie Den to rent new releases they hadn't seen in the theater. He had scored five on their "must watch soon" list, and they had planned to spend the afternoon and evening catching up.

"All right," Leo said into the phone. "We're on our way."

Sighing again, Piper moved toward the closet to get dressed. Even though she sometimes complained about not having a normal life, she wouldn't neglect her Charmed duties. A delay in video watching would cost them a few dollars in late fees they couldn't afford, but to postpone vanquishing a demon might cost someone's life.

"So what's the story?" Piper asked when Leo hung up.

"The alarm went off at P3," Leo said. "Darryl

wants us to meet him there."

Piper felt the blood drain from her face. Though she was relieved that her expertise as a demon fighter wasn't required, she was stricken with a different kind of panic. The Halliwell finances were stretched so thin that a loss of business or extra expenses would break the bank.

"Was anything stolen?" Piper's eyes widened. "Or wrecked? What if the damage is so bad that the club can't open tonight?"

"The alarm just went off," Leo explained. "Darryl hasn't arrived at P3 yet."

"I don't believe this." Piper yanked a pair of pressed jeans off a hanger.

"It's broad daylight on a Friday afternoon, Piper," Leo said patiently. "I'm sure everything is fine."

"Not possible," Piper retorted, fuming. "Either P3 has been vandalized or robbed or both" —She paused to emphasize her point— "or my new, very expensive, state-of-the-art security system went off for no reason."

Paige stepped into the dim interior of Hawk's General Store and winced when the screen door slammed closed behind her. The elderly man sitting behind the counter jumped.

"Sorry," Paige said with a sheepish shrug. "I didn't mean to do that."

"Not a problem." The old man peered around

a display of individually wrapped beef jerky
and smiled. "An occasional jolt is the only thing
that keeps this old heart going."

Paige smiled back, charmed by the twinkling
eyes in a wizened face that looked a hundred
years old. The man's blue Kansas City Royals
baseball cap seemed out of place on long gray
hair tied back with a leather thong.

"Can I help you find something?" the man
asked.

Noting the film and disposable cameras hung
on the wall behind him, Paige shook her head.
"I'm just browsing."

"Suit yourself." The old man settled back in
his chair and picked up a newspaper. "I'll be
right here if you need me."

"Okay, thanks." Paige ambled down the narrow aisle. The high shelves were stocked with
everything from canned goods and camping
gear to souvenir shot glasses, sports T-shirts,
gardening supplies, paperback romances, and
pet products. The store also sold Native
American crafts and clothing, and the far back
corner was devoted to dusty antiques and general junk.

The screen door slammed again while Paige
was flipping through a stack of old magazines in
a wooden crate. She looked up to see a man in a
county sheriff's uniform lean against the counter
by the old-fashioned cash register.

"Afternoon, Mr. Hawk," the officer said.

"Sheriff Jefford." The old man stood up, dropped the newspaper, and folded his arms. "What can I do for you?"

Mr. Hawk's tone was civil but with a guarded edge, giving Paige the impression that he was expecting trouble.

"I need to ask you a few questions." The sheriff sounded annoyed, as though he was expecting resistance.

"You can ask," Mr. Hawk said, setting his jaw. Paige could tell that he had no intention of cooperating with Sheriff Jefford's inquiry.

"Where were you last night around nine, John?" The sheriff stared the old man in the eye.

"Closing up here," John answered without blinking. "Why?"

Paige moved into the candy aisle and paused by rows of cellophane bags hanging on hooks. She saw a dark-haired young man stop outside the screen door. The other men didn't notice him.

"Carlos Martinez up at Sierra Sojourn radioed in another complaint," Jefford said. "Apparently, someone went to a lot of trouble to scare him and the cook."

Paige perked up at the mention of the resort, wondering what had happened on the mountain. The old man asked.

"How?" John leaned forward slightly. "Just curious."

"Trees that seem to burn but don't," the sheriff said. "Furniture that moves by itself. Animal skulls soaked in blood, and a ghost wolf."

"Imagine that." An amused half-grin compressed the wrinkles around the old man's eyes and mouth. "Maybe they did. Imagine it, I mean."

"Carlos doesn't have an imagination." Unperturbed by John's cavalier attitude, Jefford pressed. "Who did it?"

"Wasn't me," John said evenly.

"Not you personally, perhaps," Sheriff Jefford conceded. "Do all the Sinoyat have alibis?"

When the young man quietly slipped into the store, Paige watched without drawing attention to herself. Tall, muscular, and tanned with short black hair, he went directly to the shelf of automotive supplies and picked up a quart of oil. Like her, he pretended to be indifferent, but he was listening intently to the old man and the sheriff.

"Most of us are still in Kansas"—John Hawk's steely gaze tracked the young man a moment before shifting back to the sheriff—"where the federal government sent the tribe after they kicked us off the mountain. That was over a hundred years ago. The Sinoyat are almost extinct now."

"I know the history, John," Jefford said.

I don't, Paige thought, hoping the old man would keep talking. Her gaze fastened on a package of assorted tropical fruit lollipops that looked really good. Before she realized what she was doing, she thought about buying it. Sparkles of light flickered as the package orbed into her hand.

Hoping nobody had noticed, Paige clutched the bag and executed a wide-eyed scan of the store. She caught the young man staring at her and looked away a split second after he averted his gaze. She was pretty sure he had just been checking her out and hadn't seen the magical transfer. She *was* a girl, and he *was* a guy.

A totally cute, tall, dark, and brooding type, Paige thought as she stole another glance his way. He was absorbed in reading the label on a bottle of windshield wiper fluid, as though that would fool her into thinking he hadn't been curious about her.

"There are at least thirty of you here in Lone Pine River," the sheriff continued, referring to the Sinoyat.

John nodded. "More or less."

"Right. And you're the only people in town who have a problem with that resort up there." Jefford placed his hands on his wide belt and impatiently shifted his weight. "I just can't *prove* that you've been sabotaging Sierra Sojourn—yet."

Paige saw the young man scowl at the sheriff. Like her, he thought the sheriff was being too hard on the elderly clerk. However, the old guy had no trouble defending himself.

"I wouldn't be so quick to blame the Sinoyat

people, Sheriff Jefford." John's impudent demeanor turned serious. "Maybe Glooscap and his brother, the wolf, have returned to stop Mr. DeLancey from defiling our stolen tribal lands."

The young man by the automotive supplies rolled his eyes and looked away from the counter.

"It's a better bet that whoever is pulling these pranks will make a mistake and end up in jail. I'm watching you, John. All your tribal friends, too." The sheriff stormed out, shaking his head in frustration.

Paige frowned, remembering her conversation with Phoebe the night before. Based on her research, Phoebe suspected that there might be something sinister about Vista Recreation's newest project. Still, she hadn't had a clue whether the problem might be human or supernatural in nature.

In spite of what she had just overheard, Paige still couldn't answer that. Something *was* wrong on the mountain, but between burning trees that didn't burn, stolen tribal lands, and somebody called Glooscap who hung out with a wolf, the culprit could be anyone or anything.

Chapter

4

Paige sat by the window in the front seat of the bus, staring at an endless panorama of rocky canyons and green forest. The paved road was badly in need of repair, but that hadn't hampered their steady progress.

Only half the size of an ordinary bus, Sierra Sojourn's Mountain Express was superior to its city cousin in other ways. According to Jeremy Fenton, the Vista Recreation public relations rep and tour guide, the gray-and-green transport had been modified to handle steep, winding inclines and dirt access roads that could turn hazardous in stormy weather. With a citizens band radio, seat belts that few had bothered to buckle, and a first aid kit, the bus was equipped to deliver its passengers safely.

The shock absorbers could be improved, though, Paige thought as the vehicle lurched over a pothole. She glanced at Phoebe, who was sitting beside her.

Phoebe had stopped doodling and was absently tapping her pencil on her notebook. She seemed to be listening to Jeremy Fenton, but since his running monologue was too dull to command such rapt attention, Paige assumed her sister was thinking about Cole or the photo assignment.

Standing in the aisle a few feet back, the PR rep held on to a seat to steady himself. Slim and cocky, in his late twenties, with perfect hair, Jeremy was an upwardly mobile nerd in macho-man clothing. Everything he wore—from his gold wristwatch to khaki cargo pants—boasted a designer logo.

Paige sighed. The PR rep had started talking before the bus had left the café parking lot. An hour had passed, and he was still hard-selling the corporation as an innovative, environmentally friendly business that cared more about people than the bottom line.

"Vista has plans to build a fully equipped hotel eventually," Jeremy went on, "but not until Sierra Sojourn has established itself as the ultimate in wilderness adventure vacation resorts."

"But there are cabins, right?" A pretty young woman with brown hair cut blunt just below her ears turned to the bearded man sitting beside her. Her tanned tummy was visible between a short pink baby tee and low-slung jeans. With

seashell designs on her blue, manicured nails, a
beaded choker necklace, and a flawless com-
plexion, she was the most youthful member of
the press party. "We won't be sleeping outside or
in tents or anything, will we?"

"No, we won't, Gloria." David Stark, a
reporter for a Los Angeles newspaper, smiled
tightly. In his forties, with a scar on his left
cheek, he was an unlikely match for his young
and flashy female companion.

Phoebe had introduced Paige to several people while they were waiting to board the bus,
but she had already forgotten most of their
names. There were twelve other people in the
press party. With a few notable exceptions, such
as Mitch Rawlings, Phoebe, and Angie, the
reporters and photographers usually covered
outdoor sports, recreation, or travel events. Sally
and Jim Orlando hosted a cable TV travel show
and had already bonded with three journalists
from Europe. Gloria was the only tagalong guest
other than Paige. The young brunette obviously
didn't have any wilderness experiences, either.

"Tents are an option," Jeremy said only half
in jest, "but Phase One is complete." He
directed his next comment to Gloria. "For those
of you who haven't read the information in the
press kit we provided, Phase One includes
guest and staff cabins, endurance and skill
courses, and a community building called the
Lodge. All the modern conveniences you might

find useful, if not necessary, are in the Lodge."

"What conveniences?" Gloria frowned. Jeremy's subtle taunt had eluded her completely.

"Electricity, bathroom facilities, radio communications, food—"

Gloria paled as Jeremy listed all the amenities civilized people took for granted. David noted Gloria's reaction with an amused smile.

Paige shifted position to whisper in Phoebe's ear. "Why didn't you warn me about the lecture?"

"It wasn't listed on the schedule." Phoebe spoke softly from the side of her mouth. "If you hadn't wanted to sit up front, we could be hunkered down in the back, reading a book. Mr. Perky PR Person would never have noticed."

"Yeah, well"—Paige cleared her throat—"I get motion sickness if I sit in the back of a bus."

"Uh-huh." Phoebe glanced at the bus driver, then back at Paige. "Sure you do."

Ben Waters, the young man Paige had seen in Hawk's General Store, worked for Sierra Sojourn as a maintenance man, trail guide, and bus driver. He had driven the new bus to Lone Pine River from Vista Recreation's corporate headquarters in San Francisco that morning. If he had caught the real meaning in the exchange between her and Phoebe, he wasn't letting on. He kept his hands on the wheel and his eyes on the road.

As oblivious to everything around him now as

he's been for the whole trip, Paige thought, squirming. It had been foolish to think Phoebe wouldn't notice her interest in the darkly handsome hunk in the red plaid shirt and scruffy jeans. She just hoped the reason for her quick claim on the front seat hadn't been as transparent to anyone else, especially to Ben Waters. She had planned to draw him into casual conversation, a ploy that had been effectively foiled by Jeremy's nonstop patter.

"We'll be operating with a partial staff this weekend, but don't worry." Jeremy patted Gloria's shoulder, a reassuring gesture she returned with a coy, come-on look. "They are all in charge of their respective departments and experts in their fields."

Even Jeremy's smile has a condescending quality, Paige realized when he caught her eye. She pretended not to notice. She'd rather spend the weekend being ignored by Ben than pursued by such a plastic phony.

"So William DeLancey gets a twofer," Mitch said.

"Twofer?" Angie asked, puzzled. She was seated on the aisle, next to Mitch.

"Meaning what, Mr. Rawlings?" Jeremy asked curtly.

"I'm a little confused, too." Phoebe turned to regard the famous reporter. She was only curious about Mitch's strange remark, but her interest evoked a flirtatious smile from Mitch and a cold, jealous stare from Angie.

Poor Mitch, Paige thought with a shudder. The people on the bus had barely been introduced, but the personal plots were already taking some intriguing twists and turns.

"Your people will get to work out the bugs on us," Mitch explained with a wave of his arm, "and Sierra Sojourn will get a ton of free publicity."

"Good publicity, I trust," Jeremy said as though he expected nothing less.

"That depends, doesn't it?" Mitch grinned, deliberately putting the PR man on the spot.

"The Sierra Sojourn experience isn't for the faint of heart," Jeremy countered. He immediately launched into a description of the strenuous survival activities that would be available to the journalists that weekend.

Phoebe closed her notebook and leaned over to put it in the camera bag at her feet.

"Can I use that?" Paige asked quietly.

"Sure." Phoebe handed over the notebook and pencil, then leaned back and closed her eyes. "If anyone asks, I'm still listening."

Since Jeremy apparently did not intend to shut up any time soon, Paige couldn't try to get Ben talking without being rude. She hadn't had a chance to tell Phoebe about John Hawk's strange conversation with Sheriff Jefford, either. She decided to write it down while the incident was still fresh in her mind.

One thing is certain, Paige thought as she

opened the notebook to a clean page. *Given how this trip had been going so far, Piper and Leo are probably having a lot more fun.*

Piper's irritation grew as she flipped through the pages of the police report. The whole day had gone downhill from the moment she and Leo had gotten Darryl's phone call.

Half an hour after hanging up, they had arrived at P3 to learn that someone *had* broken into the club. The incident wasn't as disastrous as she had imagined, though. The new security system had worked, and the only damage was a broken window and a dented cash register. Nothing seemed to be missing. Apparently, the would-be thief had fled the scene empty-handed when the alarm had gone off.

Piper was annoyed because it had taken her two hours to determine that nothing had been stolen. Then she and Leo had spent another hour at the station filling out the report. By the time they finally finished and went home, twenty-five percent of their weekend alone would have been wasted.

Piper scrawled her signature on the last page and leaned back in the hard chair. She glowered across the desk at Darryl when he reached for the stapled papers. "Can we go now?"

"Are you angry?" Darryl frowned, perplexed. "At me?"

"He's just doing his job, Piper," Leo said. "It's

not Darryl's fault someone tried to rob P3."

"You should see the paperwork I have to do every time I investigate a crime." Darryl picked up the report. "You're going to need this if you want your insurance company to pay for the busted window and cash register."

"I know." Piper pouted. She hated it when she was upset and someone correctly pointed out that she was indulging a misguided emotional response. She knew Darryl wasn't to blame for the break-in or for the bureaucratic delays.

"She didn't mean it," Leo offered, trying to smooth things over.

"I can make my own apologies, thank you." Piper managed a tight smile. "I really am sorry, Darryl. It's just that, since Phoebe and Paige are both gone this weekend, Leo and I were going to spend a lazy afternoon together. Just the two of us, you know?"

"I get the picture." Darryl stood up. "We're almost done."

"Almost done?" Piper nearly exploded. "We've inventoried the club, answered dozens of questions, and filled out all these stupid forms. What else can you possibly need from us?"

"It's more a matter of what you need from me," Darryl said evenly.

"What does that mean?" Leo asked.

Darryl lowered his voice and held up the file.

"For one thing, I'll try to avoid having *this* land on the captain's desk."

Piper understood the inspector's concern. She certainly didn't want to draw attention to all the other crime files that mentioned or involved one of the Halliwell sisters or P3.

"But what if he does get curious?" Leo asked, worried.

"This is a pretty routine complaint so I don't think there's a problem, but if I'm wrong"— Darryl looked at Piper—"how long can you keep someone—immobile?"

"If they don't go to pieces, not long enough," Piper quipped, assuming he was joking.

"Just checking." Darryl grinned. "If you'll hang for a few minutes, I'll get you a photocopy of the report for your insurance company."

"Can't you just mail it . . . ?" Piper's words trailed off as Darryl disappeared down the hall.

"Give the man a break, Piper," Leo said. "He's doing us a favor."

"You're right, Leo." Faking a smile, Piper tried to look relaxed. On any other weekend, she wouldn't have minded all the hassle over a broken window and an almost-theft at the club. "Would you get me a drink of water?"

"Sure." Leo squeezed her knee, then walked over to the water cooler in the far corner.

Piper rubbed her temples and closed her eyes. She had adapted to the responsibilities of being the oldest sister-witch better than she had dared hope after Prue died. The pressure was sometimes crushing, but she handled it.

Most of the time, Piper thought. Now she could feel the tension building within her. She needed to fall back, regroup, and recharge, which meant she desperately needed the sister-free, demon-free weekend to just unwind and enjoy being with her husband. It didn't seem like too much to ask of the mysterious powers that filled out the Charmed duty roster.

"The machine was out of root beer, Matt!" a boisterous man's voice said. "I hope orange is okay."

Startled, Piper opened her eyes.

In the same instant, a police officer with a cardboard tray full of soda cans and sandwiches bumped into the corner of Darryl's desk. He lurched slightly, upsetting the balance of the shallow box. As he reached to grab the soda cans that toppled to the right, he tipped the tray to the left.

Plagued by taut nerves, Piper reacted on instinct when the sandwiches rolled off. Her hands shot out, and the sandwiches exploded into bits of paper, white and rye bread, lettuce, tuna salad, Swiss cheese, and roast beef, which splattered her clothes, face, and hair.

Clutching a can of orange soda, the officer looked around just as Leo walked up.

Leo stared at Piper aghast. "What happened?"

"Hi, honey." Piper wiped a glob of mayo off

her cheek. "This young man just dumped his lunch in my lap."

"It was an accident." Mortified, the officer stumbled over his words and stopped a rolling can of soda with his polished shoe. "Honest."

"An accident?" Leo looked pointedly at Piper.

"Of course! I'd never *deliberately* wear roast beef and Swiss without horseradish." The tension in and around Piper snapped when she started laughing.

Phoebe checked her watch as the bus plowed through the ruts in the dirt road. They had left the paved potholes several miles behind. If her calculations were right, they would reach Sierra Sojourn in about forty-five minutes. She had slept fitfully during the last hour of Jeremy's rambling orientation speech. Now that he had stopped talking and taken a seat, she was wide awake.

Phoebe glanced at the notebook Paige had stuffed in the camera bag, wondering what her youngest sister had been writing so furiously. Since Paige was dozing, she didn't disturb her to ask.

"It's starting to rain," Gloria said.

Phoebe glanced back as the young woman leaned across David to peer out the window. The reporter opened one eye, looking a bit perturbed.

"Not possible," Jeremy said, annoyed. "Our

weather sources predicted clear skies for the entire weekend."

Phoebe eyed Jeremy with guarded disdain. He acted as though the faulty forecast were a deliberate attempt to sabotage Vista Recreation's perfect PR weekend.

Gloria sat back and frowned at Jeremy, who sat across the aisle one row up from her. "What if the bus breaks down?"

"It won't." With his arms folded across his chest and his left foot propped on his right knee, Jeremy oozed confidence. "But there wouldn't be anything to worry about if it did. Ben would just call Sierra Sojourn on the CB, and Carlos would send someone to get us in the Jeep."

"But a Jeep only holds five people, right?" Gloria scanned the bus, counting heads. "We'd have to make a bunch of trips to get everyone to the resort."

Phoebe wondered if Vista Recreation had booked Gloria to provide comic relief. Mitch, Angie, and the other reporters seated nearby were all following the conversation with amused anticipation, too.

"Which means," Gloria continued, "that some of us will be stuck in a broken-down bus in the middle of nowhere—maybe for hours."

"Stop fretting, baby." David yawned and straightened in his seat. "I'm sure these people have plans for dealing with emergencies."

Phoebe quickly faced front so the reporter

wouldn't see her smother a laugh.

Paige had awakened from her nap. She nudged Phoebe in the side, mouthed the word "baby," and rolled her eyes.

"Absolutely correct, Mr. Stark," Jeremy said. "We've taken every precaution, but we're completely prepared to deal with the unexpected. Take Ben, for instance—"

"Gladly," Paige muttered in a voice so low, only Phoebe could hear.

"He's a Native American and quite proficient in matters of wilderness survival," Jeremy explained. "Right, Ben?"

Ben raised his hand to acknowledge the question. "We'll get where we're going."

Gloria waved to get the driver's attention. "Can you make a fire by rubbing wood together like they do in the movies?"

"Leave the man alone so he can drive, honey." David made the suggestion with a pointed glance outside. "That rain is really starting to come down hard."

"You're no fun." Annoyed, Gloria slumped in a pout. "So far, this isn't exactly the cool weekend break from college you promised, Dad."

Dad? So the campus cutie is the reporter's daughter, Phoebe thought with a grin. She suspected that the girl's quirky personality would wear on adult nerves as the weekend progressed. Still, it was really sweet that David Stark had brought her on the trip.

Paige leaned forward and rested her arms on the metal divider behind the driver's seat. "How long have you been working for Vista Recreation, Ben?"

Nobody could ever accuse Paige of being shy, Phoebe thought. It wasn't difficult to understand why she was attracted to Ben Waters, though. He radiated a dark mystique, an aura of depth and turmoil that reminded Phoebe of Cole. As she well knew, inner torment packaged with dark hair, dark eyes, and a handsome profile was an irresistible combination.

"A couple of weeks." Ben's manner was abrupt, but his voice had a deep, melodious quality. He gave Paige a quick look before turning his attention back to the road.

"A new guy, huh?" Paige plunged ahead without pause. "What did you do before that?"

"Law school." Ben turned on the headlights and windshield wipers. Dark clouds had obscured the sun, and the steady rain had become a deluge within the space of a few minutes.

"Really?" Paige exclaimed, impressed. "Where?"

"Princeton." Downshifting, Ben tightened his grip on the steering wheel. "I graduated last semester."

Surprised, Phoebe blurted out, "You graduated from Princeton Law School? Then why are you driving a bus?"

"Good question," Paige agreed. "I bet Ben has a good answer, too."

Ben leaned forward when the windshield began to fog up. He flicked on the defrost fan. "I thought an outdoor summer job would be a nice change of pace after hitting the books so hard for so long."

Paige nodded. "Makes sense to me."

"What about the bar exam?" Phoebe asked. "Don't you have to study for that?"

"Yeah, but I won't be taking it for a few months." Ben slowed the bus to take a sharp curve.

"So"—Paige hesitated, her eyes narrowing thoughtfully—"what did you make of all that weird stuff Mr. Hawk was talking about back at the store?"

"Weird stuff?" Phoebe asked, not knowing what Paige meant.

If Ben knew, he wasn't talking. "Sorry, but right now I'd better concentrate on the road."

Phoebe rubbed her arms, chilled by a sudden dip in the temperature. A major storm was brewing, and Ben didn't need any distractions.

"Excellent idea." Phoebe pulled Paige back into the seat. "Not a good time to talk."

Having broken the ice, Paige didn't argue. She wiped the fog off the window and pressed her face against the glass. "It looks like this storm is going to get a lot worse before it gets better."

"At least we'll have a warm fire and a dry log cabin waiting at the end of the line," Phoebe said.

"Throw in a hot spiced cider and the right company, and I'll be happy." Paige smiled, watching Ben.

Phoebe settled back to ride out the storm. Streams of water sheeted on the windshield, reducing Ben's visibility to near zero. The drone of the engine was lost in the distant rumble of thunder, and a dim glow lit up the fog when lightning struck somewhere ahead. The deep ruts and hard ridges in the dirt road dissolved into mud.

Angie gasped when the bus slid around a winding turn on the slick surface. "Shouldn't we pull over until this blows over?"

"I don't think so," Jeremy said, his voice quavering. "The bus might get bogged down in the mud. What's your opinion, Ben?"

"Better to keep moving." Ben downshifted again and steadied the wheel as the bus crawled up an incline.

"Good call, Ben," Mitch said. He gave Phoebe a reassuring nod when she glanced over her shoulder. Angie was staring out the window and missed the exchange.

Phoebe noted that the other journalists were taking the storm in stride. *Their reaction isn't all that remarkable*, she realized. Most of them were veterans of risky outings. They had climbed sheer, treacherous cliffs, ridden white-water rafts, and outrun a stampeding herd of crazed bulls in Spain, among other things. Phoebe suspected that they thrived on the danger as much as on photographing or writing about their adventures.

Over lunch Mitch had mentioned that David Stark had once parachuted into a remote jungle location with a group searching for lost treasure. They had escaped that wilderness with their lives, the tattered shirts on their backs, and a great story, but no Aztec gold.

"Is that a bridge up there?" Paige pointed out the windshield. The outline of the low, wooden trestle bridge was hard to see in the driving rain. "It looks kind of old."

"It's been here awhile," Ben said.

"It's much stronger than it looks," Jeremy quickly added. "The company reinforced the entire structure so it could handle the weight of heavy construction equipment. It's perfectly safe."

As the bus moved onto the bridge, Phoebe glanced past Paige out the window. A crude lattice of large timbers formed the sides of the rustic bridge. Through the spaces between the wooden beams, she could see the river below. Rushing water churned in whitecapped eddies around large boulders and outcroppings of rock.

A bolt of lightning split the gray gloom and slashed through the trunk of a large tree on the bank behind the bus.

Gloria screamed.

Angie grabbed Mitch's arm.

A woman in the back snapped shots of the charred, smoking tree with a high-speed camera.

Paige grabbed the metal divider.

Startled by the explosive crack, Phoebe jumped forward. She reached for the divider to stop herself from sliding off the seat but touched Ben's shoulder instead.

The vision hit with all the power and fury of the storm, overwhelming Phoebe with raw panic.

A flash flood smashed into the bridge, collapsing the wooden framework. Caught in the middle of the structure when it buckled, the bus was battered by broken timbers and thrown against jagged rocks as it was swept away. . . .

Phoebe emerged from the premonition with one terrifying image lingering in her mind.

When the twisted remains of the bus finally settled to the bottom of the river, no one had escaped.

Chapter
5

Paige's throat constricted as Phoebe shook off the effects of a vision that had been triggered when she had touched Ben. Something terrible was going to happen to him, but before Paige could ask what, Phoebe leaned toward the bus driver.

"Step on the gas, Ben," Phoebe said, her voice strained with urgency. "Now."

"The bridge is too slippery—" Ben started to protest.

Paige cut him off. "Don't argue. Just do it!"

Phoebe turned to face two dozen curious stares. "Listen up, people. Crash positions!"

"What do you think you're doing?" Jeremy gripped the seat in front of him, his temper flaring as the bus suddenly picked up speed. "Slow down this instant."

"Oh, my—" Shock choked off the rest of Angie's words.

Mitch looked out the window and yelled, "Everybody get down!"

All the passengers obeyed instantly, except the woman in the back with the camera. Forty, with short dark hair and a face lined from years spent outside, the photographer kept shooting.

Phoebe ducked and threw her arms over her head.

"Here it comes!" The woman snapped two more shots, then bent over the camera to protect it.

Paige stared as the river swelled into a huge, roiling wave surging toward the bridge. The bus was speeding toward the opposite bank, but there wasn't time to clear the danger zone. Seized with sudden fear, Paige orbed out just before the wall of water crushed the bridge.

Peeking under her arm, Phoebe saw the sparkling remnants of Paige's magical vanishing act. Although her sister had learned to orb in and out at will, she still didn't have total control of her flight response. Whenever an unexpected fright caught her, Paige beat an instinctive Whitelighter retreat.

A split second later the flash flood collided with the bridge.

Phoebe cringed as the sounds of devastation filled her ears. Cries of alarm were muffled in the roar of the river rushing past. Wooden beams snapped, and uprooted trees groaned. Ben swore as the lethal stream caught the bus in its watery grip.

"Hang on!" Ben hollered as he bus started to slide out of control. He raised his arm as the bus rammed into solid ground.

Expecting the worst, Phoebe was elated when the momentum of the impact hurled her out of the seat and slammed her into the metal divider. A few bumps and bruises were preferable to the watery grave she had witnessed in the vision.

Paige orbed back in as the bus engine sputtered and died. She smoothed back her hair with a sheepish grin. "That was close."

"You could say that," Phoebe said, understating the obvious.

A quick glance assured Phoebe that Ben had been too busy protecting himself from the shattering windshield to notice Paige's spectacular departure and return.

Wedged between the steering wheel and the back of his seat, Ben slowly pulled himself free. Bits of broken glass fell on the floor when he stood up. He bent over, removed the handheld CB transceiver, and flicked a switch on the console. When punching a few buttons didn't even raise static, he hit the unit with his fist.

"Dead?" Phoebe asked.

"Apparently." Ben's gaze glanced off Phoebe to settle on Paige. "Are you both okay?"

"I'm fine," Paige said. "I don't think we can say the same for the bus, though."

The sparks of mutual attraction between Paige and Ben are almost as intense as Paige's orbing power, Phoebe thought as she rubbed her bruised hip.

"Buses can be replaced," Ben observed. "Can you keep these people calm while I check the situation outside?"

"Phoebe is a whiz at making sure people don't freak out, aren't you, Phoebe?" Paige's eyes begged her sister to agree.

Phoebe sighed. It wasn't hard to guess what was on Paige's mind. Heavy rains and wind continued to pound the wrecked bus, and there might still be a danger of it being washed away. It wasn't safe for Ben to venture outside alone.

"Go," Phoebe said. "I'll take care of things here."

While Ben and Paige pried open the door, Phoebe leaned into the aisle to survey the other passengers. Her worry that someone else might have seen Paige's sparkling display was unfounded, however. Gloria was looking about with a stunned expression while the journalists checked for broken bones. A few had already shifted from life-threatening accident into business mode and were taking notes.

Neither the foolishly persistent photographer nor the distinguished gentleman sitting beside her seemed interested in Paige or concerned about their own health, Phoebe noticed.

"I do hope the camera came through

unscathed, Tracy," the gray-haired man said in a crisp, British accent. "Those last few shots should be quite remarkable."

Tracy's warm smile softened the austere angles of her face. Her accent was distinctly British, too, but without the aristocratic edge. "Am I to assume you've already composed some witty captions, Mr. Charles?"

"Quite right, Mrs. Charles," the man replied. "There's nothing like a good bashing about in a bus to get one's brain working."

"I didn't know you and Tracy were married, Howard." Steven Casey, a heavy-set, clean-cut man in his midthirties, was sprawled in the aisle. He rubbed one elbow as he pulled himself into a sitting position.

"I don't believe I mentioned it," Howard Charles remarked, looking down at Steven. "Anything broken?"

"Don't think so," Steven said. "Thank goodness I'm a staff writer for *Outdoor* and not a freelancer or I wouldn't have full medical coverage."

Phoebe glanced at Jeremy, who seemed frozen in shock. He jerked to attention at the mention of insurance.

"Is anyone seriously hurt?" Jeremy asked.

"We're fine," David Stark said. He had his arm around Gloria, who nodded with a brave smile.

Jeremy visibly relaxed as everyone reported

in. Angie thought she had a sprained wrist. Brandon Lane, a syndicated columnist from upstate New York, had a deep gash over his eye that might require stitches. No one else complained of anything worse than cuts and bruises.

"We have a fully equipped infirmary and a registered nurse at the Lodge," Jeremy said. "Those services will be provided at our expense, of course, but Vista Recreation has no liability responsibility beyond that."

"What if I need treatment your nurse can't give me?" Angie's eyes flashed with indignation.

"Your publisher signed a waiver, Ms. Swanson." Jeremy smiled. "I'm sure 415 will take care of any additional medical expenses you incur."

Phoebe sighed, but the corporation's callous precautions didn't surprise her. Any company that would legally cheat people out of their land, as Vista Recreation had done in Florida, wouldn't leave themselves open to negligence lawsuits.

"I can't even *get* to a hospital," Angie observed.

"Maybe we should worry about getting to the infirmary," Mitch said. "How far is it to Sierra Sojourn?"

Jeremy shook his head. "I don't know."

"About three hours on foot, if we cut cross-country," Ben said as he and Paige jumped back inside. Water dripped from their wet clothes, forming a muddy puddle around their feet. "Five if we stay on the road."

"We have to walk?" Gloria sounded insulted.

"If you want to get to Sierra Sojourn before dark," Ben answered evenly.

Unconvinced, Gloria pressed. "Why not just call that Carlos guy on the radio to bring the Jeep?"

"Because the CB is broken or the battery is dead and can't power it," Ben explained. "That's the first thing I checked. It's not even picking up a hiss."

"Can the bus be salvaged?" Jeremy asked.

"Not today," Ben said.

"Is there any good news?" Phoebe asked. So far, the only bright spot in the dire circumstances was that not only had Paige's disappearance gone unnoticed, no one had questioned how Phoebe had known the flash flood was imminent.

"The storm is blowing over." Paige waved toward the windows. The rain had tapered off to a drizzle, and the howling wind had subsided to a mere whisper of a breeze. "Looks like we'll be pitting ourselves against the elements a little sooner than we thought."

"I'm thrilled," Gloria huffed.

"I'm sure you're much tougher than you look, Ms. Stark." Tracy Charles paused by Gloria's seat. "You're certainly in much better shape than poor Mike."

"Who's Mike?" David asked.

"An unfortunate horse." There was no hint of humor in Tracy's expression as she explained. "The poor beast was swept nine miles down a gorge when the Rubicon River near Lake Tahoe flash flooded in 1908."

"Gross," Gloria gagged.

"Quite." Tracy snapped Gloria's picture, then turned to Ben. "Let's be off, then, shall we?"

Phoebe backed up a step to let the gutsy British woman pass. The fascinating personalities in the press party were making up for the less than auspicious opening of Sierra Sojourn.

Paige slowed her pace to adjust the duffel bag she was wearing like a backpack. Like Phoebe, the seasoned sports people had brought real backpacks, which were easy to haul over the rough terrain. Knowing this, Ben had rigged everyone else's luggage to be back-carried, too. The men wearing belts had contributed them for use on pieces that didn't have easily adaptable handles.

"Need some help?" Phoebe lifted the bag, taking the weight off the canvas straps so Paige could reposition the load.

"Got it. Thanks." Paige hurried forward a couple steps to catch up to Ben, who was leading the group through the forest.

Bushwhacking, Paige thought, recalling Mitch's terminology. Since the road curved back as it wound up the mountain, walking a relatively straight line between the stranded bus and the resort was just over half the distance. Although Jeremy had lamented the lost bus and his soon to be ruined Doc Martens, everyone else had tackled the hike without complaint.

Ben glanced back over his shoulder and raised a black walkie-talkie. He caught Paige's eye and quickly averted his gaze as he depressed the talk button. "Can you hear me, Mitch? Over."

"Loud and clear," Mitch's voice came back.

Before they had left the river, Ben had appointed Mitch to cover the rear with strict orders that no one was to wander out of sight for any reason. Anyone who got lost in the dense forest might never be found.

"How's it going back there?" Ben asked.

Paige didn't know how Mitch was doing, but things were going great from her perspective. Although Ben seemed a little shy, she was sure he was as interested in getting to know her as she was in getting to know him.

"No problems," Mitch said. "Everybody back here wants to push on."

"Roger that." Ben clipped the communication device to his belt and paused to check his compass.

Paige took advantage of the moment to absorb the beauty of her surroundings, feeling awed and a little amazed. Born and raised in the city, she hadn't expected to feel so comfortable in the wilds. *Must be a witch thing*, she thought as Ben moved out again.

"Gloria must be doing okay." Phoebe turned to look at David. Her burning curiosity was only thinly disguised by the casual remark.

Paige was more than a little curious herself. Contrary to his quiet, unassuming manner, David Stark was a rugged, world-class adventurer. It had to bother him that his daughter, who had made a point of hanging back with Jeremy, was attracted to the superficial PR wimp.

"So far she's been more interested than I dared hope," David said with a mischievous grin.

Paige and Phoebe both frowned, puzzled by the comment.

"In what way?" Phoebe asked.

"This is a twofer weekend for us, too," David said. "I've missed a lot of her life because I was gallivanting all over the globe. This couple of days won't make up for it, but it might help."

"What's the twofer part?" Paige prodded.

"She's the subject of my review of Sierra Sojourn." David grinned. "If these people can kindle Gloria's repressed primal instincts this weekend, then this place will probably be a hit with the executive city types they're hoping to attract."

"What a brilliant idea!" Phoebe exclaimed. "I can't wait to read what you write."

"Watch out here," Ben cautioned. He stopped

before starting up a rocky incline. "These loose rocks can slip right out from under you."

"Right. Falling head over heels once a day is enough." Paige's coy romantic reference went right over Ben's head.

"Please, be careful," Ben said. "I don't want any broken necks on my watch."

Paige sighed as the young guide carefully picked his way up the slope. Was Ben too dense or too preoccupied to pick up on her blatantly flirtatious signals?

Silence fell over the group as they climbed to the top of a long ridge. Hedged in by dense brush on one side and a drop-off on the other, everyone maintained a quiet vigilance as they followed Ben in single file.

Paige could almost feel the tension drain from the group when they entered a less overgrown section of forest. Large pines were spaced farther apart, and the ground was clear of tangled underbrush. A carpet of pine needles that had accumulated over decades added bounce to her step.

"Is it my imagination, or are we being followed?" Phoebe cast a furtive glance to the side as she moved abreast of Paige.

Paige looked back at the people strung out through the trees behind them. "We're being followed."

"I wasn't trying to be funny," Phoebe said, "although you get an A for deadpan delivery. I really have felt that something's been stalking us since we left the bus."

"Something or someone?" Paige's high spirits plunged. She had been so distracted by the accident and her attraction to Ben that she had forgotten that normal things weren't necessarily normal for the Charmed Ones.

"I'm not sure." Phoebe shrugged. "But if something or someone *is* tracking us—he, she, or it is doing a darn good job of staying out of sight."

"Maybe it's the ghost wolf the sheriff mentioned to John Hawk back in town," Paige said.

Ben's head snapped around before Phoebe could comment. "A wolf would steer way clear of this many people," he said. "There's no chance of an attack."

"What if it's sick? Or hurt? It wouldn't act normally then, would it?" Paige couldn't remember if she had read that somewhere or seen it on TV, but the question had to be asked.

"No," Ben conceded, "but I haven't seen any signs of a wolf. An unhealthy animal couldn't keep itself hidden that well."

"A *ghost* wolf could," Phoebe said, baiting him. She had immediately homed in on the fact that he had ignored the mystical reference.

"You believe in ghosts?" Ben asked with a skeptical half-smile.

"John Hawk does." Paige jumped on the opening to address the strange discussion between Sheriff Jefford and the elderly Native American man. Since she hadn't found time to brief Phoebe, she could close both information gaps at the same time.

"Who's John Hawk?" Phoebe asked.

"The old guy who works at the general store." Paige quickened her step to move up beside Ben. "What's with that Goose Cap person Mr. Hawk was talking about, Ben?"

"Glooscap," Ben corrected, "the Algonquian First Man. It's just an ancient myth."

Phoebe came up on Ben's other side. "I love a good ancient myth."

"Me, too." Paige looked at Ben with wide-eyed anticipation, leaving no doubt that she and Phoebe would persist until he talked.

"Okay, but I'm no expert." Ben surrendered with a nod. "According to the legends, Glooscap was the first and most powerful shaman and sachem to arise during the Algonquian tribes' primal history."

"What's the difference between a shaman and a sachem?" Phoebe asked.

"Both words are Algonquian," Ben explained. "A sachem was a wise elder and adviser who kept the oral histories. A shaman was a healer and a keeper of visions."

Paige detected Phoebe's slight reaction at the mention of visions.

Ben continued without pause. "Tribes in the Algonquian language group span the whole country. They say that's because Glooscap traveled the continent passing on the original Abenaki tribal traditions."

Paige just nodded, reluctant to interrupt now that Ben was on a verbal roll.

"Anyway, as the story goes," Ben said, "Glooscap established the rules for the natural order of the world, and he gets very angry with people who don't respect them."

"Such as corporations that build resorts on stolen tribal lands?" Paige asked.

"Maybe, if you believe the myth." Ben's brow furrowed in a fleeting frown. The tight grin and sudden change of subject that followed seemed forced. "Glooscap also gets credit for banishing mystical evil."

"How'd he do that?" Paige asked.

"He chased the demons and witches out of the forest with help from his brother, the wolf." Ben shrugged when Paige just stared at him. "You asked."

"Uh-huh." Paige forced a tight smile of her own. "So what would Glooscap do to a demon or a witch that came back?"

Ben leaned toward her, lowering his voice for dramatic effect. "Any entity that dared to return to Glooscap's territory after he threw it out would be destroyed."

"Oh." Paige slowed to let Ben move ahead as they left the stand of pines.

Ben stopped and dropped his backpack by a

small stream that cut through a narrow canyon. "This looks like a good place to take a ten-minute breather. We're about halfway."

"Works for me." Phoebe drew Paige aside, slipped out of her pack, and leaned against a large, flat rock. She waited until everyone else had trudged past to join Ben farther upstream before she asked, "Is there anything else I should know about your trip to the general store?"

"Well, yeah. I've just been waiting to get you alone," Paige said testily. "Nobody else in this bunch needs to know about unburned flaming trees and Native American uprisings."

"You are so right." Phoebe fixed Paige with her undivided attention. "Talk."

With the incident and her recently scribbled notes fresh in her mind, Paige told Phoebe everything she could remember.

"So do you think Mr. Hawk is pulling all those pranks?" Phoebe asked when Paige finished.

Paige shook her head. "No, he's too old to have done all those things himself, but the sheriff said there are plenty of other Sinoyat in town. If Vista Corporation *is* building Sierra Sojourn on land they think was stolen from the tribe, some of them could have done it."

"Maybe." Phoebe paused. "Or maybe Glooscap is totally furious because Vista Recreation has ruined the purity of this mountain."

"You think?" Paige didn't want to believe it,

but they had to consider the possibility that supernatural forces were at work.

"Well," Phoebe said, "weather prediction isn't an exact science, but that storm was kind of intense for the forecasters to miss."

"But not impossible," Paige said. "I've been rained out at the beach way too often when sunny skies were forecast."

"That's true." Phoebe rubbed her chin in thought.

Paige waited for several seconds before the suspense became unbearable. "So is this a witch mission or not?"

"Right now, I'd say not," Phoebe said. "Even if the storm and the pranks *are* supernatural in origin, saving a mountain wilderness from corporate development isn't an evil agenda."

"Oh, yeah!" Paige's outlook brightened immediately. The Power of Three wouldn't be needed to stop a mystical do-gooder.

"Time to move out, ladies!" Mitch called.

"That was a fast ten minutes," Phoebe grumbled as she slung her pack onto her back.

"And only ninety more minutes to go," Paige grunted as she adjusted her duffel pack. "All of them uphill."

Clustered behind Ben, the press party resumed the march through scrub brush and stunted trees growing at the base of the canyon wall on the right and the stream on the left.

Taking up his rear guard position, Mitch

turned and waved for Phoebe and Paige to catch up. "You're dawdling!"

"I'm stuck!" Angie had snagged her blouse on a low branch. Frowning, she tried to free herself without tearing the flimsy fabric.

"We're coming." Phoebe started to jog, then stopped with her head cocked slightly, listening. "What's that?"

Paige heard an ominous rumble a moment before the patter of loosened gravel sounded above. She looked up just as a ledge gave way, dumping boulders, smaller rocks, and grit. "Rock slide!"

"Get to cover!" Ben shouted as he urged Sally and Jim Orlando and three European journalists to race ahead.

David pulled Gloria and Jeremy under a ledge. The British couple, Steven Casey, and Brandon Lane jumped the stream and dove behind a pile of boulders near the opposite wall.

Angie had frozen in her tracks. Terrified, she resisted when Mitch desperately tried to drag her to safety. They were standing directly under tons of falling stone.

Paige assessed the scene in an instant and didn't hesitate to act. She focused on the barrage of stone and summoned her power. "Rocks!"

Infused with life-and-death urgency, Paige's ability to orb was amplified by several degrees. The boulders falling toward Mitch and Angie sparkled out.

Paige turned with a commanding sweep of her arm just as Phoebe rocketed upward to avoid being crushed.

Mitch knelt over Angie, shielding her with his body. Since his eyes were squeezed shut, he didn't see the massive stones vanish or rematerialize behind him.

Paige frantically motioned Phoebe to get her feet back on the ground as boulders and rocks smashed into the stream and the far canyon wall.

"I'm trying!" Phoebe's eyes flashed as she mouthed the words. She squinted in concentration to control her failing arms and slowly dropped downward.

Paige blew a wisp of hair off her forehead. As near as she could tell, everyone who might have witnessed Phoebe's aerial acrobatics or the stones' momentary conversion to light particles was out of sight behind, beyond, or under rocks.

No one moved until silence had settled over the canyon with the dust.

Ben jogged back into view without the TV people or foreign journalists. When Howard Charles started coughing, he immediately went to assist.

David crawled out from under his rock with Gloria and Jeremy.

Mitch jumped to his feet and extended his hand to help Angie up. "I'm really sorry, Angie."

"Are you kidding?" Angie shook dirt out of her long, red locks. "You probably saved my life. No apology necessary."

"How's your wrist?" Mitch asked.

"My wrist?" Angie blinked and moved her hand back and forth, testing it. "It must be fine. It doesn't even hurt now."

"Better have the nurse look at it, anyway, just to be sure." Mitch glanced at the rocks and boulders strewn across the canyon floor. "I can't believe *all* those rocks missed us. What are the odds of that happening?"

"I don't know, but our luck has got to be running out," Angie said, frowning. "We've just survived two potentially fatal accidents within a couple of hours."

Everyone paused to look at the angry redhead.

"Unless something happens to change my mind, I have my story angle." Angie glared at Jeremy. "I'm pretty sure that Sierra Sojourn's paying customers will want to test their endurance and survival skills without having their lives threatened for real."

While Jeremy tried to alleviate Angie's concerns with sputtered assurances, Phoebe joined Paige. "What *are* the odds?"

"Of all those rocks not hitting anyone?" Paige shrugged. "How many half-Whitelighter witches are there in the world?"

"I meant the accidents," Phoebe explained.

"I'm sure rock slides are pretty common—"

"Especially in a rocky canyon—" Paige interjected.

"But the timing is a little too convenient," Phoebe finished.

"Some really angry people could make a rock slide happen, though," Paige said. "Lots of things go *boom* without magic, and the Sinoyat tribe has a motive."

Phoebe just nodded, considering that theory.

Encouraged, Paige went on. "If someone in the press gets seriously hurt or dies this weekend, the bad publicity would put a quick end to Sierra Sojourn and Vista Recreation's development plans."

"Yeah," Phoebe said, "but that assumes that whoever blew up the mountain *knew* that the bus was going to crash and that Ben would lead us to this *exact* spot."

Paige inhaled sharply. "You don't think Ben—"

Phoebe shook her head. "No, I don't think Ben or any human has the power to conjure a storm, a flash flood, and a rock slide at will."

"So we can chalk it all up to coincidence?" Paige asked hopefully.

"Or Glooscap," Phoebe countered.

Paige couldn't deny Phoebe's logic. At the moment, she and Phoebe were witches in Glooscap's territory—in direct violation of his ancient no-trespassing decree.

The foreboding Paige had felt in Phoebe's

room the night before returned even stronger. She couldn't mask her apprehension when she voiced her next, distressing thought:

"What if Glooscap doesn't know we're the good guys?"

Chapter

6

Piper tested the water streaming from the show-erhead and turned the tap to make it hotter. Two hours of watching a hilarious Jackie Chan cop comedy with popcorn and Leo had almost erased the accumulated tension of the day. Another shower would rinse away any lingering traces of stress, the first having removed all lingering traces of the police officer's demolished roast beef sandwich.

Can't have a bad mood hanging on to spoil dinner, Piper thought as she stepped under the steam-ing spray. She didn't want to jinx the rest of the weekend by daring to hope that the worst was over, but things *had* taken a definitive turn for the better since they had left the police station.

Piper felt downright extravagent taking two showers in one day, but she reeked of spices and sweat from working in a hot kitchen. The aroma

wafting from the parmesan, tomato, and cauli-
flower casserole baking in the oven with a pep-
per roast didn't smell as tantalizing in her long
hair. *Nothing wrecks a romantic evening worse than
stinky hair*, she thought, *except maybe a horde of
rampaging swamp demons or sisters who couldn't
take a hint*.

Closing her eyes, Piper tilted her face and let
the warm water wash over her. As her muscles
relaxed, her mind wandered lazily through the
new weekend plan she and Leo had already
implemented.

Taking care of police business had scrubbed
an all-day movie marathon, so they had topped
off the afternoon by watching one of the rentals.
Since it could be weeks before they had another
chance to veg out in front of the TV, they had
decided to pay the late fees and keep the other
four an extra day. Leo had left to return the
Jackie Chan comedy to the Movie Den half an
hour earlier with promises to check for anything
else on their "must watch soon" list.

Piper poured a generous mound of herbal
shampoo into her hand and moved out from
under the spray as she lathered it into her hair. A
lot of men might not think a woman with clean,
wet hair dressed in comfy sweats was all that
attractive, but Leo didn't seem to mind. She
could wear a billowing flower-print muu muu
and serve dinner on paper plates at the coffee
table under floodlights and Leo would love

every minute because every minute was spent with her.

All things considered, Piper thought, she was an incredibly happy, lucky lady. Of course, she was going to serve her delicious dinner on fine china in the dining room by candlelight with a mellow CD playing in the background. She wasn't going to push her luck just because Leo was easy to please.

As Piper stepped back under the shower to rinse the suds from her hair, the flow of water suddenly dwindled to a trickle.

"No." Piper spun about to stare as the water dripping from the showerhead tapered off and stopped. Globs of lather flew as she shook her head in vehement denial. "No. Uh-uh. This can not be happening."

Sopping wet with a head full of soapy hair, Piper grabbed a towel, closed her eyes, and balled her fists. "Leo!"

Tapping her foot, Piper wrapped herself in the towel and counted backward. "Five, four, three, two, one—" She scowled darkly when the stream of flickering orb light appeared and coalesced into her husband. "What took you so long?"

"I was at the Movie Den checkout counter with *Mod Magic in Memphis*," Leo said.

Piper wrinkled her nose. "The reviews were terrible."

"I thought it would be good for a few

laughs." Leo frowned with a quick look around the bathroom. "What's wrong?"

"I have shampoo in my hair," Piper said dryly.

Leo blinked. "Why is that a crisis?"

"Because there's no water!" Exasperated, Piper threw up the hand that wasn't holding the towel. "You're a handyman. Fix it."

Leo frowned, looking stung. "I stopped being the Halliwell handyman a long time ago."

Piper rolled her eyes. "Right, but just because your cover got blown, and we found out you were really our Whitelighter and now we're married doesn't change the fact that you know how to *fix* stuff."

"Okay," Leo relented. "But first I have to figure out the problem. You, uh, didn't do any"— he wiggled his fingers—"did you?"

"No, I did not freeze or blow up the pipes or the water heater." Sighing, Piper sat on the toilet. "Please, hurry. My hair is getting stiff."

"Just checking. Be right back."

Piper sighed as Leo ran downstairs. He was an expert with a wrench, which was a totally good thing.

"That was fast," Piper said when Leo came back two minutes later.

"The problem wasn't hard to find," Leo said with a tight smile.

"Why do I get the feeling that's a bad thing?" Piper tensed.

Leo sighed with resignation. "The plumbing

in the house is fine, but the water main for the neighborhood broke. We won't have water until sometime tomorrow."

"I can't wait until tomorrow! I need water now!" Piper lifted a clump of her shampoo-glued hair. "What am I supposed to do about this? How am I going to finish dinner?"

Leo held up his hands in a calming gesture. "Can we put dinner in the fridge and save it for tomorrow?" he asked.

"I can, but why would I want to? We've got to eat," Piper added pointedly.

"Well, because there's a danger of leaks in the gas lines, and the police are evacuating the neighborhood," Leo explained. "So we've got two choices."

Piper reminded herself that the broken water main wasn't Leo's fault. It wasn't fair to be angry with him, and it wasn't rational to be angry at fate or a busted metal pipe.

"We can go to the shelter they're setting up at the high school," Leo continued, "or we can stay at a hotel."

Piper raised her hand. "I vote for a hotel."

"Can we afford it?"

"No, but Grams used to say that 'if life gives you nuts and you don't have a nutcracker, use a rock.'" Piper stood up and sidled over to Leo. "We've got a little wiggle room on the credit card. I can deal with an upgrade to room service and *new* movies on the pay channel for one night."

"Sounds good to me." Leo touched her icky hair and made a face.

Piper pushed his hand away. "We'd better pack."

"I'll wait on the porch, okay?" Phoebe pulled a hooded sweatshirt over her head and picked up her flashlight.

"Yep." Paige put a pile of folded T-shirts in the bottom drawer of the four-drawer chest in the austere cabin. "I'm almost done."

"Don't forget to turn out the lights." Phoebe tapped the battery-powered lamp on the narrow table under the front window. Another lamp sat on a smaller table between two bunks, which were covered with flannel sheets and heavy gray blankets. The only other furnishings were a wood-burning stove and two straight-backed chairs.

Not all the comforts of home, Phoebe thought as she slipped through the screen door, but after a long and tiring day, she would have no trouble at all falling asleep on the hard camp mattress.

Phoebe sat down on the log steps to wait. Inhaling deeply of the cool night air, she kept the flashlight off and stared into the darkness.

The journalists had arrived at Sierra Sojourn several hours earlier to the immense relief of Carlos Martinez, the resort manager. When the bus hadn't shown up on schedule, he and Harley Smith had driven the Jeep to the river and discovered the bus. Equipped with a long-range walkie-talkie, Harley, the head guide and survival expert, had tracked the group.

"No harder than following a herd of horses through a desert that was just swept clean in a sandstorm," Harley had said when he caught up to them.

Alerted to the group's progress by Harley's reports, Carlos had turned the unfortunate incident into a public relations triumph when he met them on the resort's perimeter. Rather than apologizing for the accident, he had praised their first successful exercise in mountain survival. No one wanted to dispute him.

Phoebe realized Vista Recreation couldn't have arranged a better demonstration to emphasize the purpose of the Sierra Sojourn program. The tough, unyielding attitude that Carlos projected made her uncomfortable, but she had to admire his tactics. He had brilliantly countered what might have been some extremely bad press.

Jeremy's relief upon reaching safety was almost tangible. Even Gloria, to David's obvious delight and astonishment, seemed pleased with her performance on the trail. The cross-country trek had inadvertently primed everyone for whatever ordeals Carlos had planned for the weekend.

It was the unplanned ordeals that had Phoebe worried. Such as finding out that the radio in the manager's office, their only means of contacting the outside world, wasn't working. The cause of the malfunction was unknown. At least, that's what Carlos had reported over coffee after everyone had gorged on Maude Billie's fabulous beef tips and garlic roasted potatoes.

What disturbed Phoebe the most was that something else had happened to isolate the press party.

Carlos, however, wasn't terribly concerned. During dessert, he had explained that an old-fashioned rope-pull ferry was located downstream from the bridge. Since it was stored in a cove, there was a good chance it had survived the flash flood. His plan was to ferry the Jeep across the river on Sunday, drive four people into town, and return with enough vehicles to transport everyone else.

If the ferry had survived, Phoebe thought with a shiver. The way things were going, she wouldn't put money on it.

Stricken with a sudden feeling of uneasiness, Phoebe flicked on her flashlight. She gasped when the golden eyes of a large animal were reflected in the beam.

"Let's go." Paige surged outside, letting the screen door slam behind her.

The predatory stare vanished.

"Did you see that?" Rising, Phoebe panned her flashlight across the stand of trees across the clearing. She wasn't sure she had actually seen animal eyes staring from the dark forest.

"See what?" Paige looked from side to side.

"Real wolf, ghost wolf, my imagination?" Phoebe didn't want to worry Paige for no reason, but she couldn't take the chance that something weird might be going on.

"You saw it this time?" Paige eased down the stairs to huddle next to Phoebe.

"I saw something," Phoebe admitted. Although Ben had said a healthy animal wouldn't venture too close to human haunts, she didn't sense that it was sick. It had made no noise and had not attacked. Of course, that explanation would also apply if the wolf weren't real.

"I suppose it could have been a raccoon," Phoebe said. "It's gone now."

"The forest is full of animals." Paige started up the trail toward the Lodge. "So is this ritual like an initiation?"

Phoebe did a double take. Apparently, she had missed something somewhere. "What ritual?"

"The campfire thing," Paige said. "Does anyone ever stay in the woods *without* gathering around an open fire?"

"Actually, now that you mention it, I don't think so." Phoebe smiled. "But first we have to find out what happened to the radio."

"I'll meet you at the Lodge, Dad." Gloria didn't wait for an answer. With her flashlight in hand, she bolted out the cabin door, jumped to the ground, and started up the trail. She was still annoyed because her father had insisted on spending the time after dinner unpacking and making the cabin livable.

As though that's possible, she thought in a huff. The lights were dim, the beds were hard, and she had a splinter in her finger from carrying firewood.

At first she had been appalled because the bathrooms were in the Lodge. Then she had found out that Jeremy was staying in one of the VIP rooms in the infirmary wing. Having to use the facilities gave her a totally perfect excuse to run into the cute PR exec whenever she wanted.

Gloria sighed. Her father was totally freaked about her interest in Jeremy, but at twenty-six he was the only guy at the resort who was young enough to be interesting. Since she had agreed to be her dad's guinea pig for the Sierra Sojourn article, he'd have to deal with her choice of company. In a way, she was actually doing her father a favor. She so wanted to impress Jeremy that she was determined to pass all the survival tests. Her dad didn't have to know that she hated the whole crude scene.

Intent on hooking up with Jeremy, Gloria almost didn't hear the rustling in the brush just off the trail ahead. Frowning, she paused to peer into dark shadows that were not entirely dispelled by her flashlight.

"Is someone there?" Gloria called. Then she realized that anyone intent on harm wasn't going to answer *that* stupid question. It was the kind of dumb thing people did in bad horror movies, she thought, right before they got killed.

A branch snapped behind her.

Don't panic, Gloria told herself. Although her heart was beating furiously and her skin was covered in cold sweat, she turned the flashlight beam back on the trail and quickened her pace toward the Lodge. She didn't dare run for fear she'd stumble off the path and lose her way.

Within a few seconds, Gloria realized that the forest had gone totally silent. She couldn't even hear the padding of her own feet on the dirt trail. Slowing down, she panned the flashlight in an arc from one side to the other. The beam failed to penetrate an opaque curtain of darkness that obscured the other cabins tucked in the trees.

"Forget this," Gloria muttered as she took off toward the Lodge with a reckless burst of speed. With the light beam bouncing all over the place, she didn't realize she had left the trail until several low branches clawed her face.

Frightened now, Gloria took a deep breath to calm her jangled nerves. Concentrating to orient herself, she turned to face the way she had come with the intention of backtracking to the path. When she raised her flashlight, she expected to see an empty, narrow corridor through the woods.

Instead, several shimmering skeletons drifted silently through the dark trees.

Gloria fell to her knees, screaming.

"I seem to have forgotten my pen." Howard Charles patted his jacket pockets, then stepped back onto the cabin porch. "I'll just be a moment, dear."

"No need to hurry." Tracy Charles pulled a flash attachment from her bag and snapped it onto her camera. "I don't believe this get-together is on a precise time table."

"These frontier types don't seem to be a terribly punctual lot, do they?" Chuckling to himself, the Englishman pulled open the screen door. He actually found the staff's casual disregard for exact timing to be refreshing, although he couldn't fathom being so cavalier about schedules as a matter of normal routine.

Howard heard the fluttering sound the moment he pushed open the solid door behind the screen door. Curious rather than alarmed, he reached inside and turned on the table lamp.

"Oh, my." Howard gasped.

The flutter became the thunderous beat of a thousand wings as a wave of screeching black bats swarmed toward him.

"Look out, Tracy!" Howard dropped to the wooden porch floor. He saw his wife duck and cover as he threw his hands over his head.

"Get away from me, you little beast!" Tracy

demanded in a sharp, no-nonsense tone.

Howard swatted one of the winged animals while he struggled to process the bizarre situation. He and Tracy had left the cabin just a minute before, and there had been no bats inside.

Paige stood outside the manager's office, which was across the hall from the infirmary. The building's extension hadn't been visible in the brochure picture of the Lodge, but it was almost as large as the dining room and lounge section. The nurse's room and lavatory facilities were located in the middle of the wing to Paige's right. The VIP quarters were at the far end. She hadn't seen or heard anyone during the two minutes since Phoebe had broken into the office.

"Are you almost done?" Paige whispered through the crack in the door.

"Yep." Phoebe quickly and quietly stepped back into the hall. She closed the door behind her and exhaled with relief. "That was a no-brainer."

"Yeah, well, it doesn't take a pro to break into an unlocked office." Paige shrugged. "Sorry, but compared with some of our other witchy assignments, this was pretty tame."

"Yeah, and with luck, it'll stay that way," Phoebe said.

"Meaning what, exactly?" Paige asked.

Phoebe motioned Paige to follow her into the

women's bathroom, where their presence
wouldn't be so conspicuous. "The radio was
smashed, so we may not be dealing with something supernatural."

Paige frowned. "I don't want to argue, but in
the short time that I've been a witch, we've run
into a few supernatural guys who really liked to
smash things—including us."

"I know," Phoebe said, "but we can't rule out
the possibility that people wanted the radio out
of commission."

"So we don't know anything more than we
did before," Paige said.

"That pretty much sums it up," Phoebe said,
opening the door.

The sound of intense sobbing filled the hallway as David burst in through the mess hall
door. Supporting Gloria with an arm around her
shoulders, he barged into the infirmary. "Nurse
Cirelli!"

"What happened?" Paige hurried to David's
side with Phoebe following close behind.
Gloria's face was scratched and streaked with
grime. Leaves and dirt clung to her jeans. "Did
you fall?"

Doris Cirelli rushed in from her personal quarters. She had spent several hours checking the bus
passengers to make sure everyone was all right.
No one had required more than basic first aid, but
she looked a little haggard. "What's going on?"

"Sk-k-kel-e-tons," Gloria stammered while

she gulped air and tried to control her sobs. "I s-s-s-aw sk-kel-e-tons . . . in the woods. They were f-f-floating, like ghosts."

"They weren't ghosts." Maude Billie, the cook, looked in from the hall. "They were phosphor sheens."

"Phosphor what?" Phoebe blinked.

"Lichens and bugs and stuff that glow in the dark." Maude was almost bowled over as Howard and Tracy Charles charged into the nursing station.

The British couple's hair looked as though it had been styled with an eggbeater, Paige observed. Bits and pieces of the forest floor were stuck to their clothes. Both looked terrified.

"I don't believe we've been bitten," Howard said, "but we should check to be certain."

"What attacked you?" Phoebe asked.

Paige knew that Phoebe was thinking about the wolf. They were both surprised by Tracy's answer.

"Bats!" Tracy said. "Vile creatures. I'd rather fall into a snake-infested pit than battle frenzied bats."

"Let's hope you weren't bitten," Doris said, pointing Tracy toward the examining room. "Where did this happen?"

"They flew right out of our cabin! Hundreds of them." Howard waved his arms. "Strangest thing I ever saw."

"Has anything odd happened to anyone

else?" David eased Gloria into a chair by Doris's desk.

"I thought I saw a wolf," Phoebe volunteered, "but I can't be sure. It was pretty dark."

"I saw a wolf last night!" Maude exclaimed.

"What about the wolf?" Carlos appeared beside the cook in the doorway.

"Nothing." Phoebe warily eyed Carlos, as though she didn't trust him. "I was just spooked by the shadows."

Nodding, Carlos surveyed the crowded room and frowned. "Are you all sick?"

Everyone but Paige and Phoebe began talking at once.

Once he understood the problem didn't involve food poisoning or something contagious, Carlos calmed the upset guests with the promise of an explanation. As soon as Doris finished her medical examinations, they were all to meet at the campfire as planned.

Can't wait to hear how he explains all this, Paige thought as she and Phoebe fled the chaotic scene.

Phoebe sat with her legs drawn up and her arms resting on her knees, waiting for Carlos.

Everyone on the premises had found a spot around the fire. Except for Ben, the Sierra Sojourn staff had gathered on the far side of the fire, away from Jeremy and the guests.

Ben stood off to the side by a large pine, an

enigma if Phoebe had ever met one. He had seemed totally at ease in the forest during the hike that afternoon, yet she had the impression that he wasn't comfortable at the resort.

Phoebe looked at Paige, who was trying not to be obvious about watching Ben. The sparks between the pair were flying as furiously as Howard's bats.

"I hear I missed all the excitement." Mitch sat on the grass beside Phoebe. "I never thought the infirmary would turn into a hotbed of news."

"I was there," Phoebe teased. From the corner of her eye, she saw Angie staring. The freelance reporter had finally agreed to confer about their article for 415 over breakfast the next morning, but only because Phoebe had threatened to attach herself to the reporter for the duration. Angie didn't want anything coming between her and Mitch Rawlings. Including her career, Phoebe thought.

Mitch grinned. "Did you get the investigative jump on the rest of us by accident or on purpose?"

"I was definitely investigating." Phoebe managed to maintain a serious expression for a few seconds before breaking into a smile. Not a lie, she thought. She *had* been snooping around Carlos's office.

"I see," Mitch said with a thoughtful nod. He leaned closer, brushing shoulders with her. "Funny. I thought Angie was the reporter and you were the photographer."

Phoebe held a finger to her mouth when Carlos raised his arms for quiet. He was still wearing the Australian bush hat, which he apparently thought enhanced his rugged image.

Phoebe placed her hands on the ground behind her and leaned back to avoid any more casual physical contact with Mitch. Intent on Carlos, he didn't react to her unspoken rebuff. Phoebe was having second thoughts about not inviting Angie to join them. Mitch seemed like a nice guy, but he was getting a little too friendly.

Paige tore her gaze away from Ben as Carlos recounted the events of that evening and some equally strange incidents that had tormented Maude the night before.

The only recurring theme seemed to be the wolf, an observation Phoebe kept to herself. The elusive animal had *not* attacked her when she was alone and vulnerable on the cabin porch. That could be a fluke, but she honestly didn't feel threatened. However, she was all too famil-iar with human and demonic killer instincts. The hunter within Carlos had been glaringly appar-ent when Maude had mentioned the wolf. If he saw it, he'd kill it. *Or try*, she thought.

"I am certain," Carlos said, scanning his audi-ence, "that human beings are responsible for these incidents. Hollywood doesn't have an exclusive on realistic special-effects techniques."

"You know this for a fact?" David asked. "Why would anyone go to so much trouble?"

"Vista Recreation has been dealing with an escalating situation since we started building," Carlos said. "Some members of a local tribe called the Sinoyat think this land belongs to them. They're trying to drive us out."

"Do they have a legitimate claim?" Mitch's tone bore a hint of challenge.

"Not that they can prove," Carlos replied evenly.

"That wouldn't stop your boss, though, would it?" Mitch pressed. "Vista Recreation was sued over another shady land deal, involving Tropical Trek in Florida."

"They were?" Angie looked shocked.

Phoebe raised an eyebrow. She wasn't surprised that her partner had not bothered to research the corporation or the resort. To be fair, though, Angie's angle for the article was physical fitness and travel—not a possible land swindle. *No extraneous information necessary*, Phoebe thought.

Mitch, on the other hand, may not have come to Sierra Sojourn for the fun and scenery as he had led them to believe over lunch in the Mountain High Café. He might be pursuing a much more serious story.

"Mr. DeLancey won that case in court," Jeremy said hotly. "That's old news, and no one here is really interested."

Except me, Phoebe thought.

"Case closed," Carlos said, fixing Mitch with

his hard stare. "Maude has hot drinks and snacks available in the mess hall, but I'd advise you all to turn in soon. Breakfast is at seven-thirty sharp."

"Seven-thirty!" Gloria's eyes flashed. "On Saturday?"

"Once we're open for business, breakfast will be served at five-thirty," Carlos said without cracking a smile. "Be on time or don't eat."

"Should we salute?" Paige scoffed as the manager strode back to the lodge with most of the employees. Harley had been assigned to fire-sit until the guests were gone.

Which won't be long, Phoebe thought as the group began to disperse. Angie took a step toward Mitch, then changed her mind and walked away.

Paige glanced toward the large pine, but Ben was no longer there. Disappointed, she stood up. "Think I'll grab some of those snacks in case we oversleep in the morning."

"Grab for two, will you?" Phoebe asked as she got to her feet. "I'll meet you back at the cabin."

"Mind if I walk with you?" Mitch edged closer to Phoebe as Paige left.

"Please, do." Phoebe wanted to find out what else he knew about the Sinoyat and Vista Recreation, but she had to be subtle. He wouldn't talk if he thought she was after an investigative scoop. "In case I need to be rescued from crazed bats or floating skeletons."

"Otherwise known as Native American ghosts," Mitch said as they headed for the trail.

"Gloria saw ghosts?" Phoebe's inflection betrayed her surprise, which Mitch mistook for skepticism.

"Or moonlight or lightning bugs or something else just as mundane," Mitch explained. "The mind can play tricks out here, especially in the dark."

"Sounds like Vista Recreation may be guilty of playing tricks," Phoebe ventured. "What happened in Florida?"

"Several residents tried to stop a legal land grab by suing Vista for paying under fair market value. They were all members of the Seminole Nation living on land their families had owned for generations," Mitch added.

"Really?" Startled by the Native American reference, Phoebe tried to sound casual. Was this an insignificant coincidence or an important common denominator between the two projects?

"Kind of sad, actually." Mitch sighed. "The tribe never legally incorporated the privately held lands into the reservation, which would have negated William DeLancey's legal position. Since the Seminole Nation never surrendered to the United States, there was no official record of the land *ever* having belonged to the Seminole."

"So DeLancey won the lawsuit," Phoebe said.

"The locals wanted the revenues and the jobs

the theme park created." Mitch kicked a stone. "No contest."

"Are the Sinoyat out of luck, too?" Phoebe was careful not to ask about anything Carlos hadn't covered.

"Without a treaty or some other proof of ownership, they don't have a legal claim." Shoving his hands in his pockets, Mitch gazed up at the moon. "So nothing can stop Vista Corporation from completely destroying this mountain with a modern hotel complex."

Except maybe Glooscap, Phoebe thought.

Piper stepped out of her third shower of the day and wrapped a towel around her head. Although she had managed to get out most of the accumulated shampoo, her hair still felt as though she had washed it in cement.

Bad hair isn't the end of my problems, Piper thought as she belted her robe and turned out the bathroom light. When she and Leo had tried to get a room at the nearest reasonably priced motel, they had discovered that two huge conventions were being held in San Francisco over the weekend. There wasn't even an outrageously expensive hotel room available in the whole city.

Three hours and many, many miles later, they had finally checked into an old one-story motel on the outskirts of the San Francisco suburbs.

"It's not even remotely romantic," Piper muttered as she flopped on the double bed, "but it's cheap, and the shower works." She was so glad to have clean hair and a place to lie down, she was not going to complain about the lumpy mattress or the pillows that refused to fluff.

Sighing, Piper picked up the TV remote and turned on the set. The police had rushed them out of the house so fast, they hadn't had time to bring the videos. *No biggie*, Piper thought. The gas and water problems would be fixed overnight, so they'd have the whole day tomorrow to watch the rental movies.

But they wouldn't be watching a movie tonight, Piper realized as she flicked through the channels. Their motel didn't provide a pay channel.

When the phone rang, Piper answered, knowing there was a high probability that Leo was on the other end. He had taken the cell phone when he had left forty-five minutes ago to find some edible takeout. "I have good news and bad news, Leo. What's yours?"

"Maybe you'd better go first," Leo said with a distinct note of caution in his voice.

"Okay, the TV works, but there are only six channels, one of which is devoted to city government. Consequently, our program options are severely limited." Piper didn't pause to take a breath. "I vote for the network comedy show that's just starting, but if you *really* want to watch sitcom reruns, a news magazine, or an analysis of the week in sports, I'm willing to make a deal."

"Comedy sounds perfect," Leo said. "Do you want to laugh with a mouth full of tacos or burgers?"

"Those are my only choices?" Piper grimaced.

"The only choices within a fifteen-minute radius of the motel." Leo sighed. "Sorry, honey, but it's so late, nothing else is open."

"It's a Friday night!" Piper glared at the phone in disbelief. "Don't people in the 'burbs party till they're starved?"

"Probably, but they settle for tacos or burgers," Leo retorted calmly.

"Tacos," Piper said, sighing. "With lots of super-hot sauce and a side of jalapeños."

"Be there in twenty." Leo made a kissing noise into the phone and hung up.

Piper replaced the receiver, leaned back with another long sigh, and turned up the volume on the TV. There were worse ways to spend a Friday night than eating cardboard tacos in a cheap motel with a man she adored.

"Like what?" Piper wondered aloud. "Waiting on tables at P3 because a waitress called in sick at the last minute certainly qualifies." She punched the pillow into a semblance of fluffy and then curled up. "And I'd much rather be here listening to this hotshot young actor tell lame jokes on TV than trying to vanquish some hotshot demonic fiend."

Yawning, Piper glanced at the digital alarm clock on the nightstand. It was just after midnight. She was surprised at how tired she was considering how late she had slept that morning. Still, between the club and the trials of being a witch, she had been pushing the envelope of endurance lately. She could sleep for a month and not catch up on her missing z's.

When her eyelids started to droop, Piper didn't fight it. She drifted off, believing that Leo would wake her up.

Phoebe was lost.

Where was Mitch?

The dark forest shifted around her, even though she hadn't moved since the moon had blinked out. *Better move now*, she thought when a branch grabbed at her sweatshirt.

A wisp of shining smoke glided through swaying trees off to one side. She turned to get a better look but saw nothing.

Another wisp drifted overhead and was gone when she raised her eyes, but she couldn't shake the feeling that she was being watched. Wary and alert, she glanced back.

A man wearing buckskin leggings and brandishing a spear sped toward her through trees that parted to let him pass. Twigs and feathers were entwined in tangles of long black hair that fanned out behind him, and slashes of paint cut white diagonals across his bronze face.

Phoebe's gaze met glittering black eyes for the briefest of moments, and a bitter cold seeped into her bones. She turned to run, but her feet wouldn't move. Terrified, she tried to call her sisters, but she had no voice. When a wolf howled, she—

—jerked awake with a gasp.

Breathless and clammy with sweat, Phoebe clutched the gray blanket under her chin. Several seconds passed while she settled her rattled nerves and dealt with the frightening reality of the dream. The experience had been similar to a vision, only much more intense. As her own breathing calmed, she heard other heavy breathing in the room.

Paige.

Phoebe turned on the lamp between the bunks. Her sister was lying on her side, facing the far wall. Phoebe watched the gentle rise and fall of Paige's blanket as she slowly became aware of other eyes watching her. Her breath caught in her throat when she turned her head.

The wolf sat on the floor at the foot of her bed. His gray coat was tinged with black and silver that paled to white around his muzzle.

Phoebe stared, transfixed by the wolf's golden eyes until he suddenly became a blur of silver-gray speed. She cringed, raising her arms to protect her face from flying glass as the animal sprang toward the window.

The lamp went dark.

Silence.

Phoebe grabbed her flashlight off the night-stand and jumped when the camp light flickered back on. Her eyes adjusted quickly to the dim glow that illuminated the cabin.

No wolf.

No open door.

No broken window.

Phoebe hugged her knees to her chest, wondering if she had really awakened from the dream this time.

Chapter
7

Phoebe paused on the porch to peer into the dense woods that surrounded the cabin. Squirrel chatter and birdsong broke the early morning stillness. In the light of day, the forest did not look nearly as ominous as it had when she had returned from the campfire the night before.

Or in my never-ending dream, Phoebe thought with a shudder.

Troubled by too many unanswered questions, she had not slept well after the visit from the wolf. Was the animal real or a spirit? Had she been dreaming or not? Was the dream a message from the ancient entity, Glooscap, to get off his mountain? Why had Vista Recreation built resorts on tribal lands in two states on opposite sides of the country? Did the corporation or William DeLancey have a hidden agenda or was it just a coincidence?

Paige had gone ahead to the Lodge a few minutes before. She hadn't been much help in interpreting Phoebe's dream experience. "I need a massive infusion of coffee before my sluggish brain can formulate any plausible theories," she said.

Recalling Paige's words, Phoebe smiled. She could use a jolt of caffeine, too.

Knotting the sleeves of a lightweight jacket around her waist, Phoebe started up the trail toward the Lodge. A faint mist hung in the mountain air, and the cool morning temperature was invigorating. The serenity of the wilderness setting took the edge off her nervousness. She had walked quite a distance before she realized that the trail was not taking her toward the Lodge, but deeper into the forest.

Since Phoebe had not left the path, the path must have changed course.

To test her theory, Phoebe turned around. The trail behind her had disappeared, replaced by a thick stand of trees, rocks, and brush. She tried to step to the side. A boulder that had not been there a moment before blocked her way. Something supernatural was definitely happening. She just had to figure out what.

The same bitter cold she had felt last night enveloped Phoebe again.

She was being watched.

In the forest ahead, she could just make out the vague outline of the man she had seen in her dream. Adorned with twigs, vines, and feathers, his black hair hung in thick tangles past his waist. Tan buckskin leggings and bronze skin provided perfect camouflage in the woods. Even the white paint on his cheeks, the stones, shells, and animal teeth on multiple necklaces, and the crude flint tip on his spear blended in. Only the glint in the fathomless depths of black eyes hinted at the supernatural power he wielded over the natural world.

Glooscap, Phoebe thought with absolute certainty, but she didn't have a clue if he was friend or foe.

Then the wolf emerged from the dense thicket in front of her, his fangs bared in a snarl.

Paige finished her second cup of coffee and glanced at the time. Only twenty minutes had passed, but Phoebe should have arrived at the mess hall by now.

Paige looked at Carlos sitting at the next table. He was watching the clock, too. Anyone who wasn't in the food line by eight would be out of luck until lunch.

Paige glanced toward the buffet setup, where Maude and Kyle were dishing generous portions of scrambled eggs, sausage, bacon, and fried potatoes onto passing plates. Angie and Mitch had just picked up trays and silverware, so they hadn't detained Phoebe on the trail. In fact, Angie was supposed to have breakfast with

Phoebe to discuss their *415* article. Judging from Angie's animated discussion with Mitch, Paige figured the redheaded reporter didn't care if her photography partner was a no-show.

But Paige knew that Phoebe wouldn't skip the meeting on purpose. Gil had taken a chance when he had given her Prue's freelance photography assignment, and Phoebe would do her best to fulfill the obligation.

Paige grabbed her Danish and left her cup and dish for the waitress to remove. Maybe Phoebe was so upset about the phantom wolf she had seen—or dreamed—last night, she had totally forgotten about meeting Angie. Not probable, Paige thought as she left the Lodge, but preferable to the alternative explanations.

Worried, Paige munched the Danish and walked down the trail toward the cabin without paying much attention to her surroundings. She didn't realize that the forest was erasing the path behind her until she noticed that none of the guest cabins were visible in the overgrown forest. Even stranger was the path in front of her. It ended about three feet away.

"Phoebe!" Paige called, but there was no answer.

Although Paige resented being manipulated by an unknown force in the weird woods, she had no choice but to follow the self-blazing trail. When she finally saw Phoebe through the trees, she checked her relief and advanced cautiously.

"Stop right there, Paige." Phoebe spoke without turning around.

Paige halted six feet behind her. Even though Phoebe had told her about the wolf, she was shocked to see the gray beast standing just beyond her sister.

"He looks real to me," Paige whispered.

Phoebe nodded. "So is Glooscap."

"He's here, too?" Startled, Paige scanned the woods on either side. She didn't see anything that resembled the fierce warrior Phoebe had seen in her dream, which was apparently coming true, Paige thought.

"He left." Phoebe's tone was clipped, as though she was afraid any loud sound or sudden movement might prompt the wolf to attack.

Not gonna happen, Paige decided. "If you move aside, I can orb the wolf away. Then we can escape—"

The wolf tensed, its tail twitching.

"No." Phoebe didn't take her eyes off the animal.

Paige understood Phoebe's reservations. They couldn't outrun the wolf, but she could keep orbing it out of their way until they reached the Lodge. "Don't worry—"

Phoebe cut her off. "He's not going to attack."

"You don't know that," Paige argued.

"I'm still in one piece," Phoebe countered.

Paige frowned at the wolf, but its yellow gaze was fastened on Phoebe. "For how long? It's got very big teeth, and they're aimed at you."

"I could be wrong," Phoebe said, "but I think we've been sent here to help the Sinoyat save this mountain and reclaim their tribal lands."

"Oh." Paige didn't disguise her skepticism or curb her sarcasm. "So that's why the ancient ghost guy and his furry little brother trail-napped us in broad daylight. Because he wants our help."

"I said I wasn't sure," Phoebe snapped with a quick glance back. "I just think that if we want to prove our good intentions to Glooscap, we can't use our powers against the wolf."

"What if Glooscap is evil?" Paige wasn't convinced the wolf was harmless, but she decided to humor her sister. If it did attack, Phoebe could levitate out of harm's way and she could orb.

"Well—" At a loss for a reply, Phoebe seemed to deflate.

Paige started when the wolf suddenly bolted into the forest and vanished. The path reappeared behind her and led right up to the porch of their cabin, twenty feet away.

"Next time we go camping," Paige said, "let's go to a forest where the trails and the trees stay put."

"There won't be a next time," Phoebe muttered. "I hate camping."

Piper peeked through the center split in the motel window's curtain. When Leo rounded the corner balancing two cups of coffee and a paper plate piled with doughnuts, she opened the door.

"Let me help." Piper took the plate and carried it to the nightstand. She picked up the bag of cold, uneaten tacos and dropped it into the metal wastebasket.

"Thanks. I almost dropped those on the way back here." Leo set down two disposable cups full of hot coffee he had gotten from the motel office. He pulled napkins, a plastic spoon, packets of sugar, and powdered creamer out of his shirt pocket. "The complimentary carry-out breakfast doesn't come with complimentary trays to carry it in."

"If that's the worst, we're set for the rest of the day." Piper sat on the bed, picked up a glazed doughnut, and scooted over to make room for Leo.

"Let's not tempt fate," Leo said. "Those are the last of the free doughnuts."

"At least we cashed in before the freebies ran out," Piper quipped. "I'm starved, and we have food. I'll take that as a good sign."

"I thought you liked living dangerously," Leo said.

Grinning, Piper turned on the TV. She had checked while Leo was gone and found a local channel that was showing his favorite old cartoons.

"Hey!" Leo pointed at the TV set. "I love those guys!"

"I know." Piper took the coffee he handed her and snuggled into the crook of his arm.

Settling back, Leo sipped his coffee and sighed with satisfaction. "So, this didn't turn out so bad, did it?"

"No," Piper agreed, drawing out the word and adding, "not unless you mind missing dinner *and* takeout tacos at midnight."

Leo frowned. "So you're mad at me for not waking you up?"

"I'm not mad," Piper insisted. Actually, she *was* annoyed because Leo had let her sleep. She had just wasted one of their two nights alone together driving around the county looking for a place to sleep and sleeping. However, she didn't want to spoil the remainder of the weekend being petty. "I've had more sleep in the past two nights than I have in the past two weeks."

"Good, because I don't want to spend the rest of the weekend in the doghouse." Smiling, Leo glanced back at the TV screen and laughed.

Piper tried to watch, but the comical antics of two mice trying to steal cheese without being caught by the big, bad house cat just couldn't hold her attention. For some perverse reason, now that she and Leo had temporarily escaped from Phoebe and Paige, she couldn't stop thinking about her sisters.

"Did you get that?" Angie nudged Phoebe's arm.

"Yes, I did." Phoebe's voice was tight as she lowered the camera. If she hadn't gotten the shot of Harley, Tracy, and Hans Gruber, the German journalist, rappelling down the side of the low cliff, Angie would have ruined it.

"It helps if you don't jostle the photographer's arm," Paige said with an impish grin.

Phoebe looked over as Paige logged the shot in her notebook, writing down the date, time, location, and names of the subjects. She didn't know how Prue had kept track of her photo information, but the system she had devised on the fly should work.

"Come on, Angie." Mitch hurried over as Harley, Tracy, and Hans safely hit the ground.

"Come on where?" Angie beamed her dazzling smile at Mitch.

"We're next," Mitch said. "Harley's orders. I'll walk you to the top of the cliff."

"What for?" Angie asked uncertainly. Snug jeans and a long-sleeved knit top that flattered her trim figure, plus hiking boots and a knit cap created an image of outdoorsy style and expertise. But looking the part and playing the part were two different things, Phoebe thought when Angie balked.

"Your article will be a lot more convincing if you're writing from the perspective of having actually done these stunts," Mitch explained.

"Right," Angie agreed. "That's why I can't wait to hit the obstacle trail this afternoon."

"Suit yourself." Mitch turned to Phoebe. "The view from the top of the cliff is spectacular. You can also see most of the complex. You can get a great shot of the solar arrays on the Lodge roof."

"I'm game."

As Phoebe moved to go with Mitch, Angie changed her mind. "But you'll have to wait your turn," she said.

Caught off guard, Mitch didn't argue when Angie linked arms and led him away.

Phoebe exchanged an amused glance with Paige. She didn't have anything against Angie, except that she was impossible to work with. The freelance reporter had finally found time to talk about photographs for the article when Carlos was dividing the press party into two groups after breakfast. The gist of the short conference boiled down to: anything that would appeal to people who were serious about staying fit; cool scenery; and don't skimp on the film.

Phoebe appreciated having the latitude to use her own judgment, and she had planned to shoot as many pictures as possible. However, Angie had been micromanaging since they had been assigned to Harley Smith. A crusty, middle-aged guy with no sense of humor, Harley was almost as hard to like as Angie, but Phoebe suspected that Carlos wasn't a barrel of laughs, either. Much to Paige's disappointment, Carlos had sent Ben to check the status of the rope-ferry on the river.

"I'm going to try to reach Leo again," Paige said when Mitch and Angie were out of earshot. "While everybody's preoccupied."

"Good luck." Phoebe glanced at Harley as Paige slipped into the woods. The guide gathered his ropes and gear and waved Mitch and Angie to follow him into the woods. They would hike to the top of the cliff by an easier, gently sloping route.

It was clear after the brief encounter with the ancient Native American presence and the wolf that morning that she and Paige needed more information, and their only means of communicating with the outside world was by trying to call Leo.

So far, that plan had been a complete flop. Mitch had decided to hang out with the 415 team, resisting Angie's efforts to pry him away. In addition, Carlos had given strict orders that no one was to wander off alone, and Harley had been watching everyone like a hawk. Getting away to "call" the Whitelighter had been difficult.

"Where's your sister, Phoebe?" Harley called down from halfway up the incline.

"Right there!" Phoebe pointed into the woods behind a rock formation, out of Harley's line of sight. "Don't ask embarrassing questions!"

Phoebe exhaled with relief when the gruff man turned his attention back to the climb.

She and Paige had each tried to reach Leo

once before. Separating from the group had been easier during their first lesson at the Lodge. Framed displays of local plant specimens with informative text hung on the walls around the fireplace. Intent on his brief rundown on what was edible and what wasn't, Harley hadn't noticed when Paige ducked outside. She had returned to hear him warn the group that they would be getting just a glimpse of the survival programs Sierra Sojourn would offer regular customers. He had strongly advised that no one sample the forest forage without checking with him first.

Phoebe had eluded Harley's watchful gaze during his "how to find shelter" demonstration, but Leo hadn't responded to any of their attempts to summon him.

Shifting back into photographer mode, Phoebe positioned herself near the base of the cliff to get some shots of Angie and Mitch coming down.

"Isn't Leo supposed to be on call twenty-four/seven?" Paige asked coming up behind Phoebe.

"Sort of," Phoebe said. "No luck?"

"Not a sparkle," Paige replied. "Did we forget to pay our Whitelighter long-distance bill or something?"

Phoebe shook her head. "He usually hears us in an emergency."

"Maybe this isn't an emergency."

Phoebe frowned. "Maybe not. Our lives aren't exactly in come-right-this-minute-or-we'll-die danger."

"Unless we count Mitch's crush on you," Paige said with a grin. "Angie's jealous fits are entertaining, but I really don't want to know how Cole reacts to a romantic rival."

"Cole promised to stay away," Phoebe said. She felt a twinge of guilt because she had encouraged Mitch's attentions so she could pick his brain. Still, it wasn't fair to let Mitch think she was available when she wasn't.

Besides, ditching Mitch might improve her working relationship with Angie, Phoebe realized. She raised the camera to capture her partner coming down the mountain. If the self-centered, obnoxious reporter didn't feel that she was competing for Mitch's affections, she might lighten up.

Paige shielded her eyes and looked up. "I think Angie's flunking form."

At the top of the rock face, Angie hung halfway off the rim on her stomach. Harley was standing beside her, ready to shove off. Mitch said something that apparently convinced the reporter to go for it. Phoebe started snapping pictures just before Angie squealed and began to slide down the rope.

Angie wasn't particularly graceful, but Phoebe had to give her credit for trying. The *415* editor wanted a travel piece with a physical fitness angle and pictures to go with it.

"Especially this one," Phoebe muttered. She caught Angie in mid-arc with her red hair flying and her knit cap falling against a backdrop of blue sky and treetops. "Perfect."

Paige sprawled in the wooden Adirondack chair on the cabin porch. Exhausted and freshly showered after surviving Harley Smith's introduction to wilderness living, she just wanted to take five with the setting sun before dinner.

Most of the journalists were having cocktails at the Lodge, but she wasn't in the mood for shoptalk about Sierra Sojourn. She and Phoebe had not been able to contact Leo. So, although they hadn't seen Glooscap and the wolf again, they were still clueless about the significance of the contacts. They could be in mortal danger, Paige thought, so she had no desire to listen to Gloria gush about Jeremy's knack for catching fish with string and a safety pin.

Phoebe had her photography assignment to offset the unnerving supernatural mystery. At the moment she was at Angie's cabin, making a duplicate list of the shots she had taken that day. Angie had gotten downright chummy after Phoebe had mentioned how much she missed her boyfriend, Cole.

Mitch had been disappointed, but Paige was sure he'd get over it. Apparently, Angie didn't mind being his second choice as long as she finished first.

Suddenly restless, Paige stood up and stretched. When she saw Ben moving through the trees, she threw all caution to the wind.

"Hey, Ben!" Paige jumped down from the porch and waved. "Got a minute?"

"Is there a problem?" Ben walked toward her, carrying a toolbox.

"No, no problem." Paige couldn't remember ever meeting anyone who was as resistant to casual conversation as Ben Waters. He waited for her to continue, and an awkward moment passed before she figured out something to say. "How's the ferry?"

"Working," Ben said.

"Oh." Paige nodded. "Did you just get back? I didn't see the Jeep at the Lodge."

"I ferried it across the river this afternoon," Ben explained, pausing again.

"Why?" Paige asked, perplexed. Without the Jeep, they'd have to hike three hours to reach the ferry.

"It feels like rain." Ben shifted the toolbox into his other hand. "If it storms, we can raft people across the river, but I didn't want to risk having the Jeep stranded on this side."

"Anxious to get rid of us?" Paige teased. Her eyes widened when she saw the swirling light of Leo orbing in behind Ben. His timing couldn't have been worse, Paige thought as she grabbed Ben's arm and urged him to start moving up the trail. "I hope not because . . . because I'm just *fas-*

cinated by all that stuff about ghost wolves and creepy primal guys."

"You are?" Ben frowned, but Paige couldn't tell if he was upset about being hauled around by a pushy female or by her reference to the myths.

Not surprising, she realized, since her words hadn't come out quite the way she had intended.

"Are you going to be around later?" Paige glanced back to see Leo dropping out of sight by the porch. "Maybe we could have coffee."

Ben hesitated, as though he wanted to accept but wasn't sure he should. "Maybe, but I've got a lot of work to do. For the opening," he added before he hurried away.

If Leo hadn't been lurking by the cabin, Paige would have followed Ben to insist. When Phoebe had told her she thought something was bugging Ben, Paige had dismissed the idea. Now she had to agree.

"Sorry," Leo said when Paige returned to tell him the coast was clear. "I thought you were alone."

"I might as well have been," Paige said. Ignoring Leo's puzzled look, she waved him back down when she heard someone else coming through the woods. When she realized it was Phoebe, she motioned him back up. "Never mind."

"Leo!" Phoebe bounded onto the porch and opened the screen door. "Where have you been?"

"Yeah." Paige stepped back as the Whitelighter vaulted onto the porch and then followed him into the cabin. "We've been calling till we're hoarse."

"You called?" Leo asked, surprised.

"Close the door," Phoebe ordered. "I don't want to explain how you got here if someone sees you."

Paige picked up the previous line of discussion as Leo gently shut the solid door. "We called every time we could sneak away from hawk-eye Harley, which wasn't often or easy." An unsettling thought struck as Paige perched on the edge of her bed. Maybe their circumstances had suddenly shifted from odd but not life threatening to extremely dire. "Are you here because we're in imminent danger?"

"I'm here because Piper has been worried about you, not because you called," Leo said.

Paige brightened. "So we're not in imminent danger?"

"What was she worried about?" Phoebe set the camera bag on the front table.

"Just a nagging feeling she had." Leo pulled the curtain closed. "It started before we left the motel, and she hasn't been able to shake it all day."

Paige raised an eyebrow at the mention of a motel but decided to stick to the matter at hand.

"So we *are* in imminent danger?" she asked,

annoyed.

"I don't know," Leo said. "Why did you call?"

"Because Phoebe is seeing things," Paige quipped.

"You had a vision," Leo said matter-of-factly. He sat in the chair by the window table and rested his arms on his knees.

"I had a dream that was like a vision," Phoebe clarified. "It was about me, and it came true—in a strange, dreamlike kind of way."

Paige listened without interrupting as Phoebe briefed Leo on everything they knew. She started with Vista Recreation's questionable acquisition of tribal lands, moved on to the encounters with the wolf and a ghostly being they thought was Glooscap, and concluded with her suspicion that they had been sent to help the Sinoyat.

"So we're stumped," Phoebe said.

"About what specifically?" Leo asked.

"About whether Glooscap is trying to run us out of the forest again," Paige said.

"More or less," Phoebe agreed. "We need you and Piper to find out if Glooscap is an evil entity we should vanquish or a champion of the Sinoyat who needs our help."

Chapter

8

Phoebe sat on the Lodge porch beside her backpack and camera bag, waiting with the other journalists to begin the long trek to the river. Paige had gone inside to thank Sonja and Kyle Larson and the Mueller twins for their outstanding service. If she were judging Sierra Sojourn solely on employee attitude and job performance, the resort would rate five stars. She wasn't the only one who thought so.

"I'll miss your cooking, Maude." Steve Casey, the heavyset reporter from *Outdoor*, shook the cook's hand and patted his stomach. "It's a good thing we aren't staying any longer or you'd be calling me El Blimpo by the end of the week."

"I'll second that." David Stark grinned, then hastened to add, "I meant the food part, not the El Blimpo thing. Maude's meals were definitely a high point of the weekend."

Maude blushed, soaking up the approval. "Did everyone get a boxed lunch? Most of you won't be getting back to the Mountain High Café until after dark."

"All set, Maude." Phoebe held up her lunch, then zipped it into her backpack. She added up the hours needed to complete the trip down the mountain: three to the river, three for the Jeep to get to town, three more back with extra vehicles, and another three hours to finish transporting everyone to Lone Pine River. Phoebe and Paige had already decided to nap as much as possible during the day so they could return to San Francisco that night. If all went well, they'd be back in their own beds before dawn.

"Speaking of high points, I thought the battle of the bats was quite stimulating," Howard joked. The British writer's opinion regarding the harrowing incident had mellowed since the attack. "Everything else has gone rather well, actually."

"You can't be serious." Angie rolled her eyes. She sat on a wooden chair with her left foot propped up. Her sock was turned down over the top of her sport shoe, revealing the Ace bandage that wrapped her ankle. "We've endured one dangerous mishap after another this weekend."

Jeremy objected. "You can't hold Vista Recreation responsible for a flash flood or a rock slide."

"No," Angie agreed, "but someone could

have warned me that snakes like to swim in
your toilets."

Jeremy flinched.

Phoebe covered her mouth to stifle a laugh.

Late the night before, Angie had gone to the
Lodge to use the bathroom. Although she had
turned on the lights, she was sleepy and not at
all alert. She didn't see the harmless black snake
rise out of the toilet until just before she sat
down. She had twisted her ankle when she
bolted out of the building and tripped on a tree
root.

Angie glared at Jeremy. "Give me one good
reason why I should recommend a resort that is
so grossly negligent and incompetent?"

All eyes turned to the flustered PR executive.

"I honestly had no idea that snakes could get
into the toilets through the plumbing." Jeremy's
regret seemed genuine.

"I wouldn't be too upset, Angie." Mitch
stepped behind the redhead and placed his
hands on her shoulders. "You're going home
with the most interesting anecdote."

"Antidote?" Gloria gasped. "I didn't know
the snake bit her!" She grimaced at the thought.

"He meant 'story,' dear." Tracy graced Gloria
with a tolerant smile, then eyed Angie's bandaged
ankle. "Will you be able to walk to the river?"

"Sure, Angie's a trooper," Mitch answered.
"Nurse Cirelli said her ankle isn't sprained. The
wrap is just a precaution."

Angie nodded with a weak smile. She obviously valued Mitch's praise above the sympathy of strangers.

No one had been happy to learn that Ben had already taken the Jeep across the river, Phoebe thought, even though his reasoning was sound. They had awakened to cloudy skies and a persistent light drizzle that was just beginning to let up.

"Is everyone ready to go?" Carlos asked as he emerged from the Lodge, followed by Ben and Paige.

Phoebe grinned as she jumped off the porch and slipped her arms through her backpack straps. Paige had fretted all night about Ben's inexplicable behavior. Phoebe didn't understand why he was so aloof, either. Shy just didn't cut it as a logical reason, not when Paige had done everything to let Ben know that she was available and interested.

As the group moved out behind Carlos, Phoebe eased between Mitch and Angie. "Are you really planning to blast Sierra Sojourn in our article, Angie?"

"Probably not." Angie shrugged, then smiled. "If we make it back to town alive, then I suppose the whole survival thing has been a success."

"Too bad I can't prove that Vista Recreation's success is built on illegal land deals," Mitch said, frowning, "but I can't publish an unsubstantiated hunch."

Phoebe wished she could help, but she didn't have any proof of corporate wrongdoing, either. The similarities between the Seminole and Sinoyat's claims were intriguing but fell way short of being conclusive.

Paige tugged on the camera bag and pulled Phoebe to the back of the line, where Ben, equipped with a rifle and a walkie-talkie, was bringing up the rear.

"Expecting trouble?" Phoebe asked.

"Carlos doesn't want to take any chances," Ben explained. "If you and Maude really saw a wolf, it's probably old or sick or injured. Either way, it's dangerous, and Carlos wants it killed on sight."

"You'd do that even if it wasn't a threat?" Paige asked.

"Don't tell Carlos, but no," Ben confessed. "Not unless it attacks. John Hawk would never forgive me if I killed a wolf for no reason."

Paige caught Phoebe's eye for a surprised second. "Are you a friend of his?"

"John Hawk works at the general store, right?" Phoebe asked.

"He owns it," Ben said, ducking under a low-hanging branch. "I've known John my whole life. He's the one who convinced me to become a lawyer."

"What did you want to be?" Phoebe didn't want to let the conversation lag now that Ben was talking.

"A lawyer." Ben grinned. "The first Sinoyat attorney in history, as far as I know."

"So then you're not just working for Vista Recreation because you wanted a break from the books," Paige said.

Don't beat around the bush, Paige, Phoebe thought. *Just go for the jugular*.

"No." Ben answered with disarming honesty. "When John told me that the tribe wasn't sabotaging Sierra Sojourn, I had to check out the place. When I pass the bar, I'll be the tribe's lawyer, so I had to know if they're innocent."

"Are they?" Phoebe asked.

Inhaling deeply, Ben hesitated. "It probably wouldn't hurt to have friends in the press," he said finally.

"Can't hurt a bit." Phoebe hopped over a puddle. The fine rain had stopped, but a lingering mist dampened clothes and spirits.

"I've been investigating for weeks, and I haven't found any evidence that implicates the Sinoyat." Ben held back to let Phoebe and Paige ease between two boulders. He caught up when the terrain widened again. "Carlos and DeLancey are assuming the tribe is guilty because of the land dispute, but that's the only basis for their accusations."

"Who do you think is doing it?" Paige asked.

"Well, unlike John Hawk, I'm sure it's not Glooscap." Ben smiled again, loosening up. "I do have a theory, though. What if Vista

Recreation is staging the pranks to weaken the tribe's legal position?"

Phoebe studied the earnest young man with renewed respect. He didn't know that John Hawk's belief in Glooscap wasn't just an old man's wishful delusion. On the other hand, she doubted that Vista Recreation was sabotaging its own project. Still, the theory gave her a jump point to probe for more information.

"What is the tribe's legal position?" Phoebe asked.

"It's hard to explain without going into the tribe's history," Ben said.

"We've got plenty of time." Paige looked at her watch. "By my calculations, we won't reach the river for another two hours and thirty minutes."

"In a nutshell, then." Ben turned sideways to maneuver down a steep incline covered with loose dirt and shale. He resumed talking as they entered a stand of tall pine. "The problem began in 1880, when the federal government convinced the Sinoyat and the Mandot to surrender most of their lands and move onto a reservation."

As Ben related his tribe's history, Phoebe realized he was sharing a verbal account that had been passed down from one generation to the next.

"The Sinoyat protested when they were forced to relocate on lands that traditionally belonged to the Mandot," Ben continued. "They had a treaty giving them possession of this mountain and the surrounding valleys, but the government refused to honor it—or even acknowledge the agreement's existence."

"Bummer," Paige muttered.

"It gets worse," Ben said. "The Mandot treated the Sinoyat as outcasts. Chief Running Wolf finally rebelled and led the tribe off the Mandot reservation and into the tribal lands the government had stolen. They held out for a couple of years before the government rounded up every surviving Sinoyat and shipped them all off to Kansas."

"Kansas?" Phoebe was shocked by the despicable treatment Ben's ancestors had received.

"That's how they felt, too, I'm sure." Ben sighed. "They were mountain people, not a prairie tribe."

"The sheriff said there were thirty Sinoyat in town," Paige said. "Is that all that's left?"

Ben shook his head. "Most of the tribe has dispersed into the general population, but several hundred usually show up at our annual tribal gatherings. John Hawk and the others who live in Lone Pine River are fighting to get this mountain back from Vista Recreation."

"If they aren't using sabotage to force the corporation out, how are the Sinoyat waging this fight?" Phoebe asked.

"In the courts," Ben said. "We have a legitimate claim based on a treaty signed by the government in 1880. We just can't prove it—yet."

"So then all is not lost." Paige smiled, anxiously accenting the positive.

"John thinks we have a chance," Ben said, shrugging. "I'm not so sure. As I said, the government has no record of the document. The tribe's copy hasn't been seen since the Sinoyat were exiled to Kansas."

"Oh." Phoebe stared at the ground. She still didn't know if the Charmed Ones had a role in the Sinoyat problem or if Glooscap was friend or foe. Twelve hours had passed since Leo had left to investigate. But if Glooscap's motives were *that* hard to figure out, the whole Sinoyat-Vista Recreation conflict might be much bigger than she had thought.

"It's not likely the Sinoyat copy survived, is it?" Paige asked, her tone and expression grim.

"It's very likely," Ben said. "Our copy is a wampum belt made of shells and bone beads, an Algonquian tradition that predates the French and Indian Wars. We just don't know if it still exists, and if it does—where it is."

"So Vista Recreation wins by default," Phoebe observed.

"Not necessarily, but this case could be the beginning *and* the end of my illustrious career as a trial lawyer specializing in Native American grievances." Ben looked up suddenly, scanning the surrounding woods.

"What?" After her previous encounters with

Glooscap and the wolf, Phoebe was instantly on edge. She sensed the animal's presence before Ben urged her and Paige to catch up to the rest of the group.

"It's probably nothing," Ben said. "It's not safe to fall behind, even if I *didn't* see something gray tracking us through the woods.

"Phoebe glanced back with a familiar, creepy feeling that the trees were closing in.

Where *was* Leo, anyway?

Piper dropped the Movie Den bag on the floor and flopped on the sofa. "That was a wild goose chase."

"We got the movies back to the Movie Den before we owed double late fees," Leo said, sitting down beside her. "It wasn't a totally wasted trip."

"Except we should have checked the library's Sunday hours before we left." Piper kicked off her shoes and tucked her feet under her. "Doesn't really matter, though. Unless the local branch carries obscure texts on American tribal mythology, we probably wouldn't have found out anything we didn't already know about Glooscap from searching the Web."

"Phoebe and Paige already knew what we learned on the Internet," Leo said.

"Right. So we've made no progress at all in twelve hours." Piper pulled a new rental video out of the plastic bag and stared at it before she placed it on the coffee table. Setting her jaw, she jumped up and headed toward the stairs.

"Where are you going?" Leo asked as Piper stomped up the steps.

Piper paused on the landing and looked down at her husband's perplexed face. "If we've got a demon to vanquish, I'd like to get it over with so we can enjoy what's left of this hopelessly messed-up weekend. I'm going to check *The Book of Shadows*."

"We've already tried that," Leo said, following her.

"I know, but I'm going to check it again," Piper said as she continued up. "Something's missing from the Charmed equation."

"Like what?" Leo closed the attic door as Piper hurried to the pedestal that held *The Book of Shadows*, the Halliwell family tome of magical secrets and spells.

"Like a page about Glooscap." Piper pointed to a blank page in the middle of the massive book. The content of *The Book of Shadows* was in constant flux. While some pages seemed to be permanent, the spells and information on others appeared and disappeared for reasons that the sisters didn't always understand. "Which I think belongs right here."

Leo looked over her shoulder at the blank page. "Maybe someone put a veil over Glooscap's bio."

"Who could do that?" Piper asked.

"Anyone with some knowledge of magic or good connections," Leo said. "Veils aren't hard to create because they just hide things. A determined demon could produce one or find someone who could."

"Then one of the Charmed Ones can probably unproduce it." Piper flipped through the book and stopped on a spell that she had not seen before. "With this."

Leo glanced at the title of the reversal spell and stepped back as Piper began to recite.

"'Pages buried 'neath a veil/Imposed by unknown foes to seal,'" Piper intoned. "'The ancient text I wish to see/Begone the veil's obscurity.'"

The pages in *The Book of Shadows* flew open to the blank page. The information on Glooscap, written in a flowing script, slowly emerged.

Piper's heart fluttered as she scanned the page. "You'd better get Phoebe and Paige, Leo."

Paige shifted position on the fallen log she was using as a bench. Although Phoebe was certain the wolf was still stalking her, the trip to the river had been danger free. Even the weather had cleared, Paige thought, looking up at blue sky laced with wisps of white cloud.

"That ferry is too cool," Phoebe said, snapping off a couple more shots, then stepping back. She sat down beside Paige and dropped the camera in the open bag on the ground.

"I've never really appreciated how resourceful the pioneers were." Paige watched as Ben and Carlos helped the cable TV couple and the three European journalists onto the crude ferry.

Measuring eight by twelve feet, the ferry was a wooden raft that floated on logs. A three-foot-high railing made of fencing planks ran along the longer sides. The ferry was moved across the river by pulling on a rope stretched from shore to shore. A second, lower rope ran through metal rings attached to the frame to keep the ferry from floating downriver. Ramps had been built on both banks so vehicles could be driven on and off.

The ferry had been built before the washed-away bridge had been completed. Sierra Sojourn had kept it as an interesting attraction. *It sure is coming in handy now*, Paige thought.

Mitch and David had helped Ben haul the ferry to the far side on the first run. Hans and the other two German men were eager to lend some muscle to the second crossing. Paige and Phoebe had waited to cross the river in the third and last group, along with Jeremy and Gloria. Since they were still hoping Leo would show, they had also volunteered to stay behind when Carlos drove Angie, Mitch, Tracy, and Howard into town.

Just then Phoebe and Paige heard a hiss coming from the forest.

"Leo?" Spotting the Whitelighter hanging back in the trees, Phoebe picked up the camera.

"It's about time," she muttered as she left to join him.

Paige cast a quick glance toward the river. Gloria was focused on the raft as Jeremy and Carlos helped Ben cast off. No one saw her follow Phoebe into the woods.

"Hurry up, Paige." Leo motioned her closer.

"What's going on?" Paige stopped short when she saw his grave expression. "Is Glooscap that bad?"

"We have to go home to find out." Phoebe slipped under Leo's outstretched arm.

"I hope Jeremy doesn't notice we've disappeared," Paige said as Leo drew her under his other arm. "For a PR guy, he's got a really low threshold for stress."

"I'd rather deal with a Jeremy freak-out than a lecture from Carlos." Phoebe's smile dissipated into a swirl of glittering light as Leo orbed.

"I'm positive we're supposed to find that treaty," Phoebe said, quickly winding up her report on the latest conversation with Ben. She really didn't want to listen to Carlos rant about stupid city people who wander off in the woods. Anxious to get back, she tried to speed up the information exchange with Piper and Leo. "What did you learn about Glooscap?"

Piper leaned forward in the old rocking chair, stopping the back-and-forth motion. "Well—"

As Piper started to explain, a disturbance in

the corner of the attic distracted Phoebe. She frowned as Cole shimmered in. The sleeve of his sport jacket was charred, and his slacks were rumpled. Dark circles of exhaustion emphasized the hunted look in his eyes.

"You look like something the cat dragged in," Piper said.

"And I thought *we* were having a bad day," Paige added. "Are you the pursuer or the pursuee?"

"Is Phoebe home yet?" Cole snapped. His humorless scowl made Paige shrink back.

"I'm right here." Phoebe slipped the camera strap around her neck and eyed him from head to toe. "What happened to you?"

"Just running for my life from Q'hal," Cole said. "Business as usual. Are you okay?"

"She's fine," Piper cut in. "But she won't be if we don't get her and Paige back to the mountain ASAP. A search party will just complicate everything."

"We have to get the scoop on Glooscap first," Paige said.

Phoebe covered Cole's mouth when he started to speak. "You'll have to catch up as we go. Sorry." Cole held up his hands in agreement.

Leo stepped forward. "Glooscap is essentially on the side of good."

"Essentially? What's with the qualifier?" Paige asked, annoyed. "He's either good or he isn't."

Leo continued. "But he follows his own rules, and his power is greater than the Power of Three."

Phoebe grimaced. "That's not good."

"That's not all," Leo went on. "Glooscap is the guardian of Native American mysteries and secrets. He won't tell you if the treaty still exists or where you can find it."

"But if we don't find the wampum belt that proves the Sinoyat own that land, Vista Recreation will wreck Glooscap's precious mountain," Paige said, rolling her eyes. "For a powerful entity, this guy is pretty dense."

"The wolf knows, too." Leo looked at Phoebe.

Cole's sardonic expression shifted to concern. "Why are you looking at her?"

"Is that why the wolf is following me?" Phoebe placed a staying hand on Cole's arm and directed the question at Leo. "Because I can find out about the treaty if I touch it."

"Don't think so!" Paige's brown eyes flashed. "Big wolf with really big, very sharp fangs, remember? And let's not forget Glooscap, who so doesn't want witches in his forest."

"Listen to your sister, Phoebe," Cole pleaded.

Phoebe understood his concern, but she couldn't neglect her duty to protect innocents. "I won't be in danger if Paige orbs the wolf to a location where Piper can freeze it."

"That should work." Piper nodded, approving the plan. "Leo can transport all of us back to the mountain just as easily as he can orb two."

"Yes, but—" Leo paused, drawing all eyes.

"What?" Phoebe asked. She had a very low tolerance for suspense, especially when her life was at stake.

"Using your powers to subdue the wolf carries another risk," Leo said.

"Worse than being shredded by wolf fangs?" Paige shuddered.

"Glooscap banished evil witches from the forest for several reasons," Leo explained. "For one thing, they used magic to steal animal souls for the purpose of gaining the animal's powers and perceptions." The stare Leo turned on Phoebe was deadly serious. "If Glooscap thinks you're trying to steal the wolf's soul, he'll kill you."

Chapter
9

"**I have** to try," Phoebe said without flinching. "A vision from the wolf may be the only way to find the wampum treaty."

Leo nodded. "I know."

Piper smiled sadly. At times like these, she understood why she loved Leo so much. His eyes reflected a deep pain because Phoebe was in danger. Yet he wouldn't shirk his duties as a Whitelighter any more than she and her sisters would deny theirs. The needs of the innocents they were charged to defend always came first. Prue had never questioned that, and she had died rather than betray the Charmed legacy.

Now Phoebe might pay the same price for the privilege of protecting the Sinoyat from— a greedy corporation? Piper frowned. The veiled page in *The Book of Shadows* wasn't the only thing wrong with the Charmed equation. They were supposed to help innocents who were threatened by supernatural evils. Instead, they were preparing to help a supernatural entity, Glooscap, defeat a mortal foe, Vista Recreation.

And who had used a veil spell to hide the facts about Glooscap?

"I hate to bring this up, but—" Piper's words were choked off when she gagged. The stench that assaulted her nostrils was so foul, her stomach roiled with nausea.

"What stinks?" Paige covered her nose and doubled over.

Cole frowned. "Nothing."

Leo wrinkled his nose in disgust. "It smells like rotten eggs and ammonia."

"Mixed with sour milk." Still holding the camera, Phoebe clutched her stomach.

"You can *all* smell something?" The puzzled look on Cole's face suddenly changed to horror. He shoved Phoebe away and cast a frantic glance around the attic.

"Watch it, Cole!" Phoebe grabbed the camera that was hanging around her neck and saved it from hitting the floor when she fell.

"What's going on?" Piper's eyes started to water as the putrid odor intensified.

"I think we're about to have a visit from—" Cole drew his arm back and threw an energy ball toward a grotesque demon as it shimmered in.

Hairless, with slimy green mottled skin, the yellow-eyed fiend looked like a cross between a horned lizard and a frog. Gold bands clamped around its neck, arms, and ankles accessorized a togalike garment woven of coarse brown grass.

"What's that?" Piper dove for cover behind a pile of pillows when the ugly, smelly intruder returned fire with a lightning bolt.

"Q'hal!" Cole jumped back, but the leather toe of his boot sizzled where the lightning bolt glanced off.

Paige and Leo squatted on either side of *The Book of Shadows's* pedestal, which offered them no protection at all.

"That's Q'hal?" Phoebe coughed. "Why didn't you warn us he was coming?"

"Or that he smells like a swamp?" Paige crawled to the window and opened it.

"Because *I* can't smell him!" Cole zinged another burst of lethal energy across the attic.

Q'hal slithered clear. Hissing and spitting in rage, he released another lightning bolt.

Cole dropped to the floor but not fast enough to completely avoid Q'hal's crackling burst of energy. The bolt singed his hair and burned a hole through the wall. "Q'hal's evil essence is masked so other demons can't detect him."

"Lucky you." Leo scrambled over to Piper.

"Not really," Cole said curtly. "If I could smell Q'hal, then I'd know when he was coming. Gotta go."

Cole blew Phoebe a kiss, hurled another energy ball, and shimmered out. The charged grenade passed harmlessly through Q'hal's fading form as he left and obliterated a box of old paperback books.

Everyone else ran out of the attic.

"I hope we have a fumigating spell," Paige said when they reached the ground floor.

"We probably do." Piper smoothed back her hair and glanced upward. "In *The Book of Shadows*."

"Can you hold your breath long enough to get it?" Paige said, sneezing, then sneezing again. "I have never smelled anything that awful before."

"Sewer gremlins come close," Leo said.

Phoebe sighed. "First we have to find the Sinoyat treaty. Then we can figure out how to deal with Cole's dump demon."

Phoebe was tense with excitement and apprehension when she materialized in the woods with Leo, Piper, and Paige. Although she couldn't see it, she knew the wolf was close. The inexplicable attraction that had drawn the animal to her in the first place had evolved into a telepathic-like bond, which was growing stronger.

"Excellent navigating, Leo." Paige glanced around the small clearing. Sunlight streamed through branches arching overhead, and beads of rainwater glittered like diamonds on emerald green leaves.

The Whitelighter had positioned them as ideally as possible, Phoebe realized. Having gotten the lay of the land on his earlier trip, Leo had chosen a spot farther away from the river. Since Phoebe didn't hear Carlos or Jeremy calling, she assumed the men were not yet aware that she and Paige were absent without permission.

"Pretty," Piper commented on the picturesque scene with an unapologetic lack of enthusiasm. She focused on Phoebe. "I'm ready whenever you are. Where's the wolf?"

Paige waited expectantly.

Phoebe closed her eyes, relying on the bond that had enhanced her intuitive senses. When the wolf brushed her awareness, a mental perception she equated with a whisper in her ear, she pointed into the woods.

Paige held out both hands. "Wolf!"

Phoebe held her breath as the wolf began to form several feet in front of her. When Piper raised her hands, she tried not to think about Glooscap's revenge if Piper accidentally turned the wolf into furry confetti instead of a temporary statue.

"Get down!" Carlos shouted.

Phoebe's head jerked toward the sound of the manager's anxious voice. She watched helplessly as events took a turn they had not foreseen and couldn't prevent.

Carlos burst out of the woods just as the wolf finished forming. Believing the animal was about to attack, he raised his rifle and fired.

Piper spun about in the same instant to freeze Carlos in midstride and the speeding bullet in midair.

The wolf, which was no longer in Piper's magical sights, turned to run. He looked back as Phoebe grabbed the suspended bullet and put it in her pocket. She locked onto the predator's golden gaze for a heartbeat before he fled.

Phoebe's hopes of helping the Sinoyat vanished with the retreating wolf, the only link to the missing treaty.

"Okay." Piper winced slightly in response to the chaotic disruption. "Now what?"

"Well, let's see." Hands on her hips, Paige shifted her brown eyes from Carlos to the woods. "Let's get the wolf back so Phoebe can read its mind while Carlos is still frozen."

"Good plan," Phoebe said, "except the wolf is gone. I don't feel him anywhere."

"The wolf might come back." Leo walked over to Carlos and peered into his squinty eyes. The glint of determination was more pronounced in the dark shadow created by the brim of his Australian bush hat. Leo stepped back with a sigh. "But I don't know what to do about this guy."

"Do you think he saw us?" Piper nervously nibbled her fingernail.

"You and Leo?" Phoebe shrugged. "Hard to say. He was sighting down a rifle barrel at the wolf, so maybe not."

"Doesn't matter," Paige said, unconcerned. "If Piper and Leo hide before he unfreezes, Carlos is not going to admit he saw two people who aren't here—not even to himself."

"Works for me, especially since we don't have any other ideas." Piper frowned thoughtfully. "How are you going to explain the wolf that isn't here?"

A sly smile crossed Paige's face as she studied her hand. "I've got an idea."

"Caaar-los!" Gloria's high voice rang through the woods.

"Phoebe?" Jeremy called. "Paige! This isn't funny!"

"Oops! Whatever you're going to do, Paige, do it now!" Piper tugged Leo's sleeve. They ran into the woods and disappeared into the shadows.

Phoebe raised the camera. Claiming she just wanted to take a few last pictures wasn't a great excuse for breaking the don't-wander-off rule, but Carlos would probably buy it.

Paige was ready when Carlos suddenly became animated. With a sweep of her arm, she orbed a large branch into the path of his running feet.

Carlos tripped and sprawled on the ground with his arms flung wide. He did not let go of the rifle, but his hat flipped off his head.

The loud retort of the gunshot, delayed when Piper froze the action, resounded through the peaceful quiet.

Paige squealed for effect, pretending to be startled.

"Carlos!" Phoebe sprang toward the fallen man as Gloria and Jeremy ran into the clearing.

"What's all the shooting about?" Jeremy demanded. A long scratch above his knee stained the hem of his khaki safari shorts red. He brushed leaves off his shoulder and muttered when he saw a dirt mark on his short-sleeved, open-necked shirt.

"It was only *one* shot," Gloria scoffed.

"The gun went off when Carlos fell," Phoebe explained.

"I was shooting at the wolf," Carlos said with pronounced indignation. Clambering to his feet, he grabbed his hat and pressed it back on his head. He rubbed his scraped elbow, but ignored the dirt clinging to his clothes.

"Where?" Gloria gasped.

"What wolf?" Phoebe looked at Paige. "Did you see a wolf?"

"No, I didn't see a wolf." Paige shook her head, then asked Carlos, "Are you sure you saw a wolf?"

"I'm sure," Carlos snapped. "It ran off, but it probably hasn't gone far." Shouldering the rifle, he jogged forward to study the wolf's tracks.

"What are you doing?" Phoebe asked, but she already knew he was planning to hunt down the wolf. One way or another, she had to put the brakes on that. The wolf was not a threat, and

Piper and Leo were still in the woods.

"I'm going after it," Carlos said bluntly.

"You're going to kill it?" Gloria darkened with the fury of the righteous. "The wolf hasn't *done* anything!"

"It will if someone doesn't stop it first," Carlos lashed out at the young woman with undisguised scorn.

"It can wait until we get these people back to town," Jeremy said. His voice held a hard edge that dared Carlos to argue.

To Phoebe's surprise, Carlos backed down. Apparently, a happy press and free publicity were more important to Vista Recreation than safety and Carlos's macho image, and Carlos knew it.

As he led the way to the ferry landing, Carlos glanced back at Phoebe and Paige. "Don't think about wandering off again, ladies. I'm giving Ben permission to confiscate your shoes if you try."

Paige saluted. "Wouldn't dream of it."

Ben was just pulling the ferry to shore when they reached the river. He jumped off and secured a rope around a metal cleat attached to the ramp.

Carlos nodded toward the far bank. "Where is everyone?"

Ben waved upriver, where the bridge used to be. "They're waiting by the Jeep. Mitch and Steven are keeping an eye on things."

"Let's not waste any time, then," Carlos said,
motioning for Gloria to board the floating plat-
form. "We've got a long day ahead of us yet."

"Remind me to put in a request for another
Jeep." Jeremy glanced upstream. The back end
of the wrecked bus was barely visible through a
tangle of bridge timbers, tree branches, and rock.
He sighed as he turned toward the ferry. "Mr.
DeLancey is not going to be happy about his
bus."

Phoebe hung back, using her senses to probe
for the wolf. She saw Ben's eyes widen in alarm
before the animal's presence registered. The
sight of the wolf sitting on the rocky bank,
watching her with riveting golden eyes, was
oddly comforting. The primal nobility of the
magnificent gray-and-silver predator reinforced
her sense of purpose and resolve.

Then Piper worked her magic. Just as Ben
started to shout a warning, he was frozen,
mouth open. Carlos and Gloria were stopped in
place on the ferry facing the far shore. Jeremy
was caught straddling the small space between
the ramp and the raft.

With Leo close on her heels, Piper stepped
out of hiding, her hands raised to freeze the
wolf.

Phoebe's gaze moved beyond the wolf to the
shadowy figure watching from the trees. With
his bronze skin, black hair, and buckskin clothes,
Glooscap blended into the forest so perfectly,

Phoebe was not sure she had actually seen him when the image faded away. But she was suddenly certain that it would be a huge mistake to immobilize the wolf.

"Don't, Piper," Phoebe cautioned.

Piper lowered her hands, shutting down her power at the last second. "I hope you know what you're doing."

Phoebe nodded. "The wolf has a free-will issue."

"As long as it doesn't involve sinking his teeth into fresh witch," Paige said with a wary eye on the animal.

Phoebe took a deep breath as the wolf stood up and padded toward her. She knew she wasn't physically at risk, but she was nervous about experiencing the mind of the wild beast. She also knew she had no choice—not if she wanted to stop Vista Recreation from turning the Sinoyat's tribal lands into a commercial wasteland.

Swallowing hard, Phoebe reached toward the wolf and stiffened when he slipped his head under her palm. She swayed, stricken by the clarity of the images flowing from the animal's mind.

The beaded wampum belt was shaped like an elongated oval with long leather thongs streaming from tapered, rounded ends. Wooden and bone beads stained red, blue, and green were combined with varying shades of brown, gray, and black stones and shells on a background of smaller, bleached bone beads. The design was simple and easy to decipher. A blue wavy line representing a river ran from a crude rendering of a wolf in the upper-right corner to the image of a lake in the lower left. Gray, green, and red fish circled the lake. The image in the upper-left corner appeared to be a mountain cliff in profile. A pine tree bent so the top touched the ground filled the lower-right corner. The center was adorned with a cluster of eagle feathers and a leafy branch.

As soon as Phoebe had cemented the appearance of the wampum belt in her mind, the images shifted. She felt an overwhelming sense of awe as she looked up into the frothing foam of a towering waterfall. Dominating the center of a huge cavern with smooth rock walls, the cascade began in midair high above her.

Phoebe was yanked back to reality when the wolf moved away, breaking the connection. She shook off the vision fog just in time to see his bushy gray tail disappear into the forest shadows. For the last time, she realized. The wolf had told her what Glooscap wanted her to know. He would not return until the mountain belonged to the Sinoyat again.

"What did you find out?" Piper asked Phoebe.

"I know what the treaty looks like, but finding it may not be easy. Depends on whether the Sinoyat's oral tradition has been handed down in accurate detail." Phoebe didn't want to discourage anyone with the fact that they might be looking for a little wampum belt in a great big mountain range.

"You'll have to fill us in later, Phoebe." Leo glanced toward the frozen people on the ferry and pulled Piper closer. "We have to go."

Paige sighed as Piper and Leo orbed out. "Sometimes life really isn't fair. They ride a white light home in all of five seconds, and we have to sit around for hours before we can drive for hours to get there."

"At least we don't have to walk." Phoebe grinned as she turned toward the frozen young lawyer. "And Ben will be with us all the way to Lone Pine River."

Ben snapped out of his paused state. "Look out—" Exhaling, he ran his fingers through his short dark hair. "Now *I'm* seeing wolves that aren't there."

"Maybe it's something in the water." Paige winked as she hauled her duffel bag onto the wooden raft.

Paige leaned back against a large boulder and stretched her legs out in front of her. She hadn't complained about her aching muscles because she didn't want anyone to think she was a wimp, but she couldn't wait to get home.

She looked up as a chorus of good-byes launched the Jeep on its journey down the mountain. Tracy and Angie waved out the windows. Phoebe waved back, then hurried over to the waiting site she and Paige had staked out for the day.

"Well, Mitch and Angie are off to Lone Pine River." Phoebe sat on the log opposite Paige and stared at the business card in her hand.

"Good. Fourteen hours and counting until I'm soaking in a hot bath." Paige arched her back and rubbed the stiffness out of her neck. "Who gave you the card? Angie?"

"Mitch." Phoebe slipped the card into the side pocket of the camera bag. "He noticed that you and Ben were getting along pretty well. He wants me to let him know if Ben says anything that might help expose Vista Corporation."

"Does Mitch know anything we don't?" Paige asked.

Phoebe shook her head. "I gave him a quick rundown on the history lesson we got from Ben, but that's not hard evidence. Mitch can't act on unsubstantiated suspicions. He can't even prove that Vista Recreation cheated the Seminole in Florida."

"If you're hoping this assignment will launch you on a new career track, why would you give Mitch your scoop?" Paige folded her arms, daring Phoebe to come up with a good answer.

"Because he's a well-known writer for a national news magazine. *Everybody* reads him," Phoebe countered. "I can't think of a better way to get high-profile publicity for a good cause."

"And?" Paige asked when she sensed Phoebe had something else to say.

"I don't think I really want a career as an investigative journalist." Phoebe smiled. "It's too much like tracking down demons and figuring out their agendas and how to vanquish them. I'd like a job that uses a different set of skills."

Ben ambled over holding one of the box lunches Maude had distributed. "Am I interrupting?"

"Nope." Paige grinned, thrilled that Ben wanted to socialize. "Pull up a rock and make yourself uncomfortable."

"Lunch!" Phoebe dug her lunch out of her backpack and opened the box. "Bottled water, two sandwiches, cookies, an apple, and two energy bars. This might hold me until we get back to the Mountain High Café."

"Maude is a treasure." Paige opened her paper napkin and placed it on her lap.

"So how well do you know this mountain, Ben?" Phoebe said, unwrapping a sandwich.

"I've walked over quite a bit of it since I started working for Vista two weeks ago. Why?" Ben twisted the cap off his water and took a long swallow.

Since they hadn't had a chance to discuss Phoebe's vision encounter with the wolf, Paige had no idea where Phoebe was headed with her questions. She bit into her apple and listened, as curious as Ben.

"I was just wondering if there are any big caves," Phoebe said. "With waterfalls over the entrances, maybe?"

Ben looked at Phoebe, impressed. "I didn't know you were a spelunker."

Paige blinked. "A what?"

"Someone who likes to explore caves," Phoebe explained. Her flashing eyes cautioned Paige to butt out. "I, uh, dabble in spelunking—sometimes. So is there?"

"A big cave with a waterfall?" Ben shook his head. "I've never seen one, but John Hawk might know. We can ask him when we get back to Lone Pine River."

"We won't get back to town until late," Paige said. "Won't he be asleep?"

Ben smiled, shaking his head. "Not with three carloads of journalists arriving at the café. Business is so scarce in warm weather, the general store will be open just in case anyone wants today's newspaper or a souvenir."

"Excellent." Nodding, Phoebe took a bite of her sandwich and chewed in thoughtful silence for a minute. "Has anyone ever searched for the wampum belt on the mountain? I mean, what if the tribe hid it before the government shipped them off to Kansas?"

"It's possible, I suppose, but"—Ben hesitated—"if they did, we have almost no hope of finding it. I'm not an expert on the oral histories, but the story is always told the same way. The treaty was lost, not hidden."

"Mr. Hawk might know about that, too," Paige said.

"He might," Ben agreed, "but locating that wampum belt is a bigger long shot than my plan to stop DeLancey."

"Which is?" Paige said, taking a sip of water.

Ben glanced from Paige to Phoebe's earnest face. If he had any reservations about trusting them, it didn't show. "It may be a fool's errand, but I have an appointment with Mr. DeLancey Tuesday morning. He thinks I want to discuss working in the firm's legal department after I pass the bar."

"But that's not what you have in mind," Paige observed.

"Nope." Ben tossed his apple in the air, caught it, and rubbed it on his sleeve to shine it. "I'm going to tell Mr. DeLancey that I'll be representing the Sinoyat and that my clients intend to tie him up in court for years."

"How will that help?" Phoebe asked, frowning.

"For starters, I can probably get an injunction to stop construction of the hotel complex." Ben sighed. "It's only a delaying tactic, though."

Phoebe nodded. "Because if you can't prove the tribe owns the mountain, the corporation will eventually get clear title."

Ben nodded. "The tribe couldn't get legal representation without forking over a huge retainer because the case is so weak. Without the treaty, the Sinoyat have no chance of beating Vista Recreation in court."

"Are you sure Mr. Hawk won't mind?" Phoebe trudged across the café parking lot behind Paige and Ben. She was glad they had locked their gear in Paige's car after arriving in Lone Pine River. She had carried her heavy backpack far enough for one day. It was after ten o'clock now, and the general store was closed.

"The lights are on." Paige pointed to a small house set back in the trees.

"Don't worry," Ben assured them as he stepped onto a low stoop by the front door. "When it comes to the Sinoyat's claim on the mountain, John will talk to anyone anytime." The door flew open as Ben raised his fist to knock.

"Come on in." John stood back to let his surprised, but apparently not unexpected, company pass. "I hope you all like plain tea, 'cause that's all I've got. The kettle's on."

"Sounds wonderful, Mr. Hawk." Phoebe smiled and followed him through the small living room into a smaller kitchen.

Shelves built into one of the living room walls were stuffed full of books. Stacks of more books were piled on the floor. Dream catchers, paintings of primitive tribal life, and other Native

American artifacts hung on the other walls. The old man also subscribed to the major news magazines, which were lying on a table by an overstuffed chair. The current issue of *National Weekly*, Mitch's magazine, was on top.

Everyone sat down in mismatched chairs around an old Formica dinette table in the kitchen. As John poured water into a teapot and set out cups, Ben brought him up to speed on recent events at Sierra Sojourn. When he finished the story of Angie's midnight adventure with the toilet bowl black snake, John burst into guffaws of laughter. "He's joking with me, right, Paige?" Wiping tears from his eyes, John sat down.

"Nobody could make up a story like that." Paige spooned sugar into her tea and stirred. "Although between the bats, Gloria's ghosts, and the vanishing wolf, the snake wasn't the most bizarre encounter anyone had this weekend."

"It was definitely a weird couple of days," Ben agreed.

The old man's eyes twinkled. "I keep telling Ben that Glooscap is angry, but he won't listen."

Ben changed the subject. "I brought Phoebe to see you because she's interested in caves, John."

"Any caves or a particular cave?" John asked.

"A very large cave with smooth walls and a waterfall," Phoebe said. "One that covers the entrance, perhaps."

John didn't have to think before he answered. "There isn't anything larger than an animal den on this mountain or anywhere near here."

Disappointed, Phoebe decided not to hold back. "Do any of your legends mention a waterfall that flows out of thin air?"

"No, but that's an intriguing concept." John studied Phoebe closely. "There's something very different about you, young lady."

"I'll say. She's always flying off on some irrelevant tangent," Paige interjected to derail the old man's train of thought. "It's very annoying, especially when people have real problems that need real solutions."

John turned his probing gaze on Paige.

Shifting nervously, Paige just kept talking. "Like the missing wampum treaty your tribe needs to prove you own the mountain."

"Do you know what the treaty looks like, Mr. Hawk?" Phoebe poured herself another cup of tea.

"Yes, it's part of our oral history." Without prompting, John described the wampum belt Phoebe had seen in her wolf vision down to the finest detail. "The designs represent the boundary landmarks. The belt is a map as well as a legally binding document."

"It's too bad the treaty was lost," Paige said.

John looked up sharply. "It wasn't lost."

"Hidden?" Phoebe asked hopefully.

Ben frowned. "I've been hearing this story

since I was a kid, John. The translation is very specific. The wampum belt was lost."

"In the original Sinoyat," John explained solemnly, "the word for *lost* was the same as the word for *stolen*."

Chapter

10

Paige walked into the kitchen holding her eyes open with her fingers. "Do we have any instant awake?"

"If you find any, I'll take two." Phoebe held up two fingers. Her eyelids drooped closed.

"If you mean coffee, there's a fresh pot." Piper looked up from her cup. "Didn't you sleep well, either?"

"Like a rock," Paige said as she slid into a chair. "For three hours. Not long enough."

"That happens when you stay up most of the night." Piper's smile oozed satisfaction. It probably wasn't fair to taunt Phoebe and Paige, but she felt entitled to a pinch of I-told-you-so. "You guys would have gotten a lot more sleep if you hadn't taken Leo's 'later' literally."

"You wanted to know what we found out," Paige shot back.

"Not at three o'clock in the morning," Piper said. "It's not like we had to act immediately to help the Sinoyat. We don't even know what to act upon."

"I do," Phoebe said, opening one eye. "The wampum treaty is out there."

Piper paused to subdue her temper. It wasn't her sisters' fault that Leo had been called away on Whitelighter business before dawn or that she had no idea when he'd get back. Nine-to-five in Leo's line of work could mean minutes or months.

"How do we know that for sure?" Paige dragged herself to the counter and pulled a mug out of the cabinet.

"Because the wolf wouldn't have shown me what it looks like if it wasn't lying around somewhere, waiting to be found." Phoebe looked at Paige. "Pour me one, would you?"

"'Finding' being the big problem," Piper said. "Got any ideas how to go about doing that?"

Phoebe flipped open the laptop computer. "I'm going to cruise the information highway and hope that some helpful hints turn up. What's on your schedule?"

"A few hours at P3 to catch up the accounts from the weekend, and then to the grocery store," Piper said, glancing up at Paige. "Did you ask for the day off?"

"No." Paige handed Phoebe a cup of coffee. "I'll get through today somehow."

"By the way," Piper said, "who is the innocent?"

Phoebe's head snapped up. "The Sinoyat?"

"The whole tribe?" Piper asked, sipping her coffee.

"What about Glooscap?" Paige said. "Can't a supernatural good guy be an innocent? Maybe he'll go 'poof' if the tribe loses the mountain to a dirty, rotten corporation."

Piper and Phoebe both paused to consider that possibility.

"Don't think so," Piper said. "Although that does raise another question: Who's the *supernatural* bad guy?"

Phoebe frowned. "Yeah, I've wondered about that, too."

Bleary-eyed from staring at a computer screen all day, Phoebe closed the laptop. She had moved into the living room to work off the coffee table after Piper had come home with the groceries. Projects involving electronics and paper notes did not fare well in proximity to Chef Piper in a culinary frenzy.

Stiff from leaning over the keyboard, Phoebe raised her arms and stretched. She was still worn out after the long drive home from Sierra Sojourn and too little sleep the night before, but she hadn't been able to take a nap. Whenever she started to doze off, she was prodded awake by the nagging feeling that time was critical.

"I'm home!" Paige slammed the front door so hard, the knickknacks on the tables rattled.

"Bad day?" Phoebe asked when Paige bounced into the living room.

"Long day." Paige leaned against the doorjamb and kicked her shoes into a corner. "Mr. Cowan was hovering over everyone like a vulture waiting for road-kill. No forty winks for the working weary today."

"Well, just so you don't feel cheated, I couldn't sleep, either." Rising, Phoebe straightened the stack of notes on the coffee table. "But my research went well."

"What about the pictures?" Paige asked.

"What pictures?" Phoebe looked up, frowning. "Oh. *Those* pictures."

"Right." Paige tossed her purse onto the upholstered chair. "The ones of Sierra Sojourn that Gil is paying you to develop and print."

"Not to worry," Phoebe said. "He doesn't need them until Friday. I've got plenty of time to decide."

"To decide what?" Paige asked as Phoebe bustled toward the kitchen.

"Whether to pay someone else to develop and print or to risk ruining the film trying to do it myself." Phoebe didn't want to discuss photography. She was bursting to tell Paige and Phoebe what she had learned about the Sinoyat's wampum treaty.

"What is that fabulous aroma?" Paige halted and closed her eyes to inhale.

Piper set a small bowl down on the counter. Her white chef's apron was splattered with red sauce, and her cheek sported a smear of gooey, yellowish gunk. Wisps of hair had escaped the large barrette clamped at her neck, giving her a happily harried look. "Spaghetti sauce with mushrooms and meatballs." Piper shook garlic powder into the bowl of yellow goo and set the large container of pungent spice aside. Then she vigorously stirred the powder into the mixture with a fork.

"Garlic powder? How come you're not using fresh garlic like you usually do?" Phoebe asked, incredulous.

"We're out, and I forgot to pick it up at the grocery store," Piper snapped, annoyed.

"What *is* that stuff?" Paige pulled a can of soda out of the fridge and perched on a stool.

Piper held up a long loaf of French bread that was still in the wrapper. "Garlic spread for garlic bread."

"How long do we have to wait to eat?" Phoebe took the top off the big pot on the stove and breathed in the savory odors of Italian spices and tomato sauce. She replaced it when Piper playfully slapped her hand. "Sorry, but I'm starved. Heavy thinking takes a lot out of a person."

"Thinking with results, I hope." Piper blew her hair off her forehead and tapped the fork on the bowl. A glob of excess garlic butter fell off the tines.

"I've made some progress." Sitting down, Phoebe gave them the abbreviated version of her findings. "I did an Internet search for 'Native American artifacts.' One site I turned up publishes a tribal newsletter that reprinted an article from a magazine called *Attic Antiques.*"

"The Sinoyat's wampum treaty is in somebody's attic?" Paige popped the top on her soda can.

"Somebody's storm cellar," Phoebe said. "Some joker named Colonel Matthew Clarke was in the cavalry troop that relocated the Sinoyat to Kansas in 1887. When Chief Running Wolf threatened to walk to Washington to shame the government into honoring the treaty, the colonel confiscated the wampum belt along with several other tribal heirlooms."

"What a jerk." Piper pulled the wrapping off the bread.

"That's an understatement." Phoebe took an orange from the bowl in the center of the table and started to peel it. "Colonel Clarke obviously didn't think the artifacts were worth anything, because he locked them in a steamer trunk and left them there for decades. Someone in the family finally opened the trunk when the farm was auctioned off thirty years ago."

"What happened to the loot?" Paige asked.

"Sold at auction," Phoebe said, "but the buyer donated everything to a museum in Kansas City, Missouri."

"I can't believe it's that simple." Piper wiped the smear off her face with a clean corner of her apron. "Even if the museum doesn't want to relinquish the wampum belt, the Sinoyat only need to borrow it to prove their claim."

"Except it's not at the museum." Phoebe tore the peeled orange into halves, spraying juice all over the table. "It was stolen along with several other unusual pieces a year ago—five weeks after the Sinoyat publicly challenged Vista Recreation's right to develop the land. They designated the boundaries of the property based on the designs woven into the belt. Because of dedicated tribal historians like John Hawk, the description has survived verbally for generations."

"Stolen? That can't be a coincidence." Piper's brow knit in a contemplative scowl as she gave the sauce a quick stir.

"No, and neither is this." Phoebe slowly dismantled the orange, making a pile of orange wedges on the table. "*Three* weeks before the theft and *two* weeks after the Sinoyat accused the corporation, the wampum belt was pictured in a catalog the museum sent to all its major patrons—including William DeLancey, CEO of Vista Corporation."

"Who must have recognized the landmark designs!" Paige slumped as the implications of Phoebe's research sank in.

"Are you thinking what I'm thinking?" Piper

set another large pot in the sink and began filling it with water for the pasta. "That *DeLancey* stole the belt so no one would connect it to the Sinoyat's claim?"

"I think that's entirely possible," Phoebe said. "The artifacts were never recovered, and the theft was just too convenient to discount DeLancey as a prime suspect."

"That makes sense," Paige agreed, "except for the fact that you're so certain the wampum belt still exists. If DeLancey stole it so the Sinoyat couldn't support their claim to the mountain, why didn't he destroy it?"

"I'm not sure, but I'll venture a guess," Phoebe said. "DeLancey makes generous contributions to museums all over the country. Maybe he just couldn't bring himself to destroy a piece of Native American art."

"So he buried it in a cave under a waterfall?" Paige asked.

"I guess that's possible, too." Phoebe wondered if she could get close enough to DeLancey to initiate a vision. The Sierra Sojourn project and all related aspects—like potential lawsuits and stolen wampum belts—would be on his mind.

Phoebe's thoughts were suppressed by Cole's unannounced entrance. He looked more bedraggled and harassed than he had the previous day. The prey rather than the predator, Phoebe thought as he finished shimmering in.

"Were you followed?" Piper sniffed the air for Q'hal's foul scent. Satisfied that Cole was alone, she finished cutting the loaf of French bread in half.

"It's only a matter of time." Cole collapsed into a chair at the table. "If I use my sensing ability, I can't detect Q'hal, but he can find me."

"So don't use it," Paige said.

"Q'hal can follow a trail that's been cold for a century." Cole reached across the table to hold Phoebe's hands. "And he knows where you live. Can you find a way to vanquish him?"

"You told me you could handle Q'hal," Phoebe said.

Cole shrugged. "I lied."

Phoebe stared into Cole's tired, haunted eyes. After the close call with Q'hal in the attic, she had meant to check *The Book of Shadows* for a spell to destroy the malodorous demon. Sleep-deprived and preoccupied with the Sinoyat problem, she had forgotten to do it. She decided that Cole didn't need to know that. "I'm sure we can conjure up something."

"Since Q'hal's got the worst case of body odor in the universe, I'm surprised he hasn't died from embarrassment." Paige grinned. "Maybe we can kill him with a deadly dose of deodorant."

Frowning, Piper stopped shaking garlic powder over the butter mixture she had spread on the split loaf of bread. Her nostrils twitched.

"In fact, we could use a giant air freshener right now." Paige's face contorted as the fetid odor of decayed meat slowly tainted the air. "Oh, gag."

Cole's chair tipped over as he sprang upright, cocking his arm back to defend himself.

Sickened by the stench, Phoebe gasped as Q'hal materialized near the stove. The slimy green demon hissed at Cole and raised his fists to strike.

"Oh, no. You're not going to stink up *my* kitchen!" Piper snapped the cap off the large container of garlic powder and doused Q'hal with the potent spice.

Cole heaved an energy ball.

Phoebe covered her ears when Q'hal shrieked. Choking and sputtering, the putrid swamp monster shimmered out.

The energy ball hurtled through the space where Q'hal's head had been, zoomed past Piper's nose, and struck the wall.

Piper stared at the smoke rising from the charred hole in the drywall and threw up her hands. "Our insurance rates are *never* going to go down."

Cole sighed. "Sorry about that, Piper, but thanks for getting rid of him."

"Yeah." Phoebe waved her hand in front of her face. "How did you know garlic powder was an effective repellant?"

"I didn't." Piper reached under the sink and

pulled out a plastic bottle of air freshener. "I just happened to have the garlic powder container in my hand. I had to do *something*." She scowled at Cole and sprayed herbal scent into the air.

"This is only a temporary reprieve." Cole picked up the fallen chair and sat down again. "Garlic may be offensive to him, but Q'hal can't ignore his blood oath. He'll be back."

Piper replaced the cap and handed Cole the container of garlic powder. "Keep this with you or you're banished from the house. Just until we defeat the stinky creep."

Cole took the garlic container and glanced toward the stove. "What's cooking?"

"Spaghetti." Relieved that Cole was safe and the house was still standing, Phoebe smiled. "Now that Q'hal knows you're armed, maybe you can stay for dinner."

"Is that on the menu?" Cole pointed to the pile of peels and orange wedges in front of Phoebe.

"Uh, no." Grossed out by the results of her nervous fidgeting, Phoebe wrapped the mess in paper napkins.

A shaft of swirling blue light appeared by the back door. When Leo emerged, he sniffed and frowned. "There's something wrong with the spaghetti sauce."

"Just a touch of *Eau de demon*," Paige said.

"Leo!" Grinning with joy, Piper threw her arms around Leo's neck. "You're home!"

"I'm just on a break." Leo pulled Piper's arms away and held her gaze.

Piper's smile faded. "For how long?"

"As long as it takes to deliver a message from the big guys upstairs," Leo said, pulling up a chair. "They have a theory about who might have instigated the Glooscap situation."

Piper set the large pot of water on the stove, but she didn't turn on the burner. She sat down by Leo.

"Someone besides William DeLancey?" Paige slipped off the stool and joined the gathering at the table.

"Someone *inside* William DeLancey," Leo said.

Phoebe blinked. "You mean the CEO of Vista Recreation is possessed? By whom?"

"By a lower-order demon that Glooscap exiled." Leo leaned forward. "Right now it doesn't even have a name."

"What's on its dastardly agenda?" Paige asked.

"It needs a willing human host in order to function," Leo said, "while it tries to establish a permanent identity. When it succeeds, it will have freedom of movement in this world and vastly improved status in the underworld."

"Did it choose to inhabit DeLancey for a reason?" Phoebe asked.

"I'm sure it did. DeLancey has sole control of Vista Recreation and all the corporation's assets." A hint of urgency infused Leo's tone as he continued. "The demon has to perform an elaborate ritual on sacred tribal land in order to achieve its goals. However, if the demon or its human host sets foot in Glooscap's territory, Glooscap will destroy them both—utterly."

Paige squinted, confused. "If the demon or DeLancey can't be on tribal land without getting blasted into oblivion, then they can't be on tribal land to perform a ritual. So what's the problem?"

"There must be a 'but' clause," Cole said. "There's an exception to every evil rule, too."

"Really?" Piper smiled smugly. "I'm so glad you evil guys aren't exempt from that."

"Ex-evil guy," Phoebe corrected.

Cole waved toward Leo. "Let's get back to the social-climbing demon with the identity crisis, shall we?"

Leo answered Paige's question. "If the demon, through DeLancey, secures possession of *all* the lands Glooscap holds sacred, Glooscap will lose the power to destroy the demons he banished. And after the demon completes the ritual and evolves, it can and will obliterate Glooscap."

"But Glooscap is stronger than the Power of Three. Why does he need us?" Piper asked. "Why doesn't he just do in the demon and get it over with?"

"Because Glooscap is confined to his sacred lands," Leo explained, "where the demon and DeLancey don't dare go."

"So we're supposed to vanquish the primal evil dude with no name," Paige said.

"You've got it." Leo pointed at Paige and stood up. He leaned over to kiss Piper.

Piper held up her hand. "Did this demon cast the veil spell over the Glooscap page in *The Book of Shadows*?"

"No, but with control of DeLancey's money and network, it could easily find someone to work that minor magic." Leo completed the kiss. "See you soon." Before Piper could object, Leo orbed out.

Phoebe quickly sorted through the deluge of information, trying to make sense of it all. They had all wondered about the absence of a supernatural bad guy. Although the demon culprit had no identity—yet—they had a target. But there were still a couple of troubling loose ends.

"So is Glooscap the innocent?" Phoebe glanced at the sober expressions around the table.

"Well, he'll be an obliterated supernatural being if we don't stop DeLancey's demon," Piper quipped, "but Glooscap doesn't fit the usual criteria for an innocent." She paused. "Neither does the collective Sinoyat."

"There must be somebody who's in the thick of this situation who's vulnerable," Cole observed. "Someone who represents the tribe."

Paige paled. "Ben."

"Has to be," Phoebe agreed.

When the tribe couldn't afford a lawyer, the Sinoyat had had no hope of getting their land back from Vista Corporation, and the demon wasn't worried. However, if Ben won the Sinoyat's case in court, the corporation could never possess all of Glooscap's territory, and the demon would have no hope of performing its elevation ritual.

"Ben has a meeting with DeLancey at Vista Recreation's headquarters in the morning." Paige looked at Piper. "I'm calling in sick tomorrow."

"To do what?" Piper asked bluntly.

"To protect Ben from what's-his-no-name," Paige countered.

"How?" Piper folded her arms. "This demon is a nonentity. There's nothing specific we can use to devise a vanquishing spell or potion."

"I guess there's not much chance garlic powder would work again," Cole said, holding up the container.

"Probably not." Piper rose to stir the simmering sauce.

Phoebe frowned, dismayed by the complications. They couldn't use magic that might harm William DeLancey, even if he was a greedy lowlife. Bringing evil humans to justice was Darryl Morris's job. But Ben would be in constant danger from the ambitious demon unless it was destroyed. *Hard to do without a spell or potion that would work*, she thought.

"Wish I could help," Cole said.

Phoebe stared at the garlic powder in Cole's hand. The spice wouldn't kill the demon living in William DeLancey's body, but it gave her a brilliant idea. "Maybe you can, Cole," Phoebe said. "Maybe you can."

Chapter

11

Paige paused while her sisters entered the rotating glass door into Vista Recreation Incorporated. Located in an expansive plaza with lush landscaping and intricate stonework, the building complex was a showcase for William DeLancey's artistic tastes.

A remarkable rendition of the solar system graced the front courtyard. Planets, the major moons, and the sun had been sculpted in stone and rested on clear, plastic pedestals. Engraved plaques on each pedestal provided the basic facts about each body and its satellites. A larger plaque set into the stone walkway notified the world that the work was based on a William DeLancey concept. Paige was confident the artist had received more than adequate financial compensation to make up for the lack of artistic credit.

The interior was just as awesome, Paige thought, looking up as she moved inside. Smooth, gray marble walls rose toward a ceiling three stories high over the spacious lobby.

Paige bumped into Phoebe, who had stopped to stare at the huge water fountain in the center of the lobby. A central spout in the middle of a shallow pool spewed plumes of water twenty feet into the air. Agitators churned the water in the pool, creating frothy bubbles.

"If you were a wolf, what would you call that?" Phoebe asked.

"A waterfall." Piper nodded toward the walls. "Gray marble."

"This could be mistaken for a huge cave," Paige said.

"From a wolf's perspective." Phoebe scanned the interior. "But I don't want to jump to conclusions."

"This is pretty conclusive, if you ask me." Piper followed Phoebe across the lobby, her high heels tapping a staccato rhythm on the hard floor. Wearing a fitted navy blue skirt and matching blazer, with her long hair rolled into a neat twist, she looked like an up-and-coming young executive.

Paige tagged behind, wondering if she should have worn more conservative attire. Both her sisters had opted for wardrobes that would blend into the business environment. Phoebe looked assertive in glasses, a gray pantsuit, pink blouse, and a print scarf in shades of mauve.

Paige glanced at her reflection in a shiny dark panel between elevators and smiled. Her long-sleeved, scooped-neck red top and short black leather skirt with high black boots would be outstanding in *any* environment. Her target audience, however, was Ben.

"So that's William DeLancey." Piper cocked her head to study the portrait of Vista Recreation's founder and CEO.

"That's him." Phoebe flexed her fingers.

Paige gazed up at the large oil painting hanging on the back wall of the lobby. In his midforties, DeLancey was handsome with steely blue eyes, salt-and-pepper hair, and a square jaw. Through the medium of paint, the artist had captured the man's intimidating, ruthless personality and cleverly suggested that he never smiled.

Worried about Ben, Paige crossed her fingers as Phoebe placed her hands on the canvas.

Closing her eyes, Phoebe swayed as images from the man's mind flowed into her consciousness. When she snapped out of the trance, she paused to calm her rapid breathing.

"It's here," Phoebe said, her voice low and strained. "He put the belt in a large vault that's full of other artifacts and valuables."

"More stolen stuff?" Paige asked.

"I don't know." Phoebe shrugged. "Do you have the magazine picture I printed out?"

"Right here." Paige pulled the picture of the

wampum belt out of her purse, but she didn't unfold it. She had every detail of the treaty memorized.

"There's Ben." Phoebe pointed toward the bank of elevators.

"A cutie, huh?" Piper grinned as Ben stepped into the elevator. This was her first glimpse of the young lawyer.

Paige nodded as the elevator doors closed. She almost hadn't recognized Ben in a suit and polished black loafers. With a briefcase in one hand and the other hand casually shoved in his trouser pocket, he had looked quite at ease for a man walking into the corporate lion's den.

"Let's go." Phoebe entered the next available elevator. She had done her homework in advance and knew that DeLancey's office was on the sixth floor.

For Paige, the swift ride upward seemed to take longer than necessary. They exited the elevator just as Ben walked into the suite of offices at the end of the hall.

"What about the recorder?" Paige whispered.

Phoebe slipped her hand into her jacket pocket. A click sounded. "We're recording."

"I'm ready." Piper raised her hands and smiled with impish glee. "We haven't done in a demon in days."

They picked up the pace and entered DeLancey's outer office just as the receptionist opened the door to the CEO's inner sanctum.

"Wait!" Phoebe called to Ben and rushed forward. "Sorry we're late."

"The traffic is just horrendous during rush hour," Piper added for good measure.

"Who are these people, Mr. Waters?" The receptionist, a pretty but proper young woman, eyed Paige with unguarded disdain.

Paige smiled. "We're with him."

"They're with me." Ben waited until the receptionist returned to her desk, then whispered, "What are you doing here, Paige?" He looked at Piper. "And who's this?"

"Piper Halliwell." Piper quickly shook his hand and spoke in her don't-give-me-a-hard-time-or-else voice. "I don't have time to explain, but we're here to help. Get inside now!"

Phoebe pushed him in the door.

William DeLancey was seated behind a large desk. His computer screen and keyboard disappeared into automated, recessed compartments when he stood up. The only thing left on the black desktop was an antique quill pen and inkwell.

"Isn't it a bit unusual to bring the secretarial pool to a job interview, Mr. Waters?" DeLancey said, arching a bushy eyebrow.

Piper and Phoebe bristled, but they kept quiet when Ben stepped forward. Phoebe nudged Paige and glanced to the left.

Paige nodded. The door to the large walk-in vault was the first thing she had noticed when they entered the room.

Two elegant wing chairs and a low table stood between her and the vault. An exquisite floral arrangement and recent editions of vacation industry magazines rested on the table. The two walls behind the desk in the corner office were mostly composed of glass windows. Two additional matching wing chairs were placed in front of the desk. The only other furnishings in the tastefully austere décor were bookcases on the wall adjacent to the vault. Leather-bound volumes shared the shelf space with select examples of modern and primitive art.

"Yes, but I'm not interviewing for a job," Ben said, not cowed by the CEO's brusque, insulting manner. "I'm here representing the Sinoyat, to inform you that the tribe will be initiating legal proceedings to secure their rightful ownership of a property you call Sierra Sojourn."

DeLancey laughed. "Don't bother, kid. I've heard the stories about the missing wampum treaty, but there's no truth to the rumor. The Sinoyat can't prove the government deeded them that land. If you're smart, you'll forget this folly and join my legal team. That's the only way you can win."

Ben smiled. "That depends on the endgame, doesn't it?"

Paige nudged Phoebe and asked softly, "When?"

"Anytime," Phoebe whispered back.

"Don't even try to threaten me," DeLancey

said with calm detachment. "The case is a loser, and you will be, too, if you pursue it."

Paige turned toward the vault and closed her eyes. She visualized the beaded treaty and muttered the command, "Wampum belt."

Since he was standing in front of the three witches, Ben did not see the brilliant orb light when the Sinoyat artifact appeared in Paige's hand.

"You can forget building a hotel complex on that mountain, Mr. DeLancey," Ben said, "because I'm going to keep you tied up in court for years."

DeLancey ignored Ben. His icy blue gaze was fastened on the belt draped over Paige's hand. "How did you get that?"

"What?" Ben asked.

Piper hit the lawyer with a focused freeze before he saw something they couldn't explain.

"You mean this Sinoyat wampum belt treaty that someone stole from a museum in Kansas City last year?" Paige raised the belt, hoping to prod the flustered body-sharing demon into a confession.

"Of course, I mean the wampum treaty," DeLancey raged. "It was locked in my vault, you impertinent little thief."

"*I* found it," Paige huffed. "You stole it."

"Yes, I did, but you and your friends are not going to live long enough to tell anyone!" the demon within DeLancey roared.

"Is that good enough?" Piper asked Phoebe as a misshapen globular form began to separate from the CEO's human body.

"I hope so," Phoebe said. "Be careful."

"Hurry." Paige stepped back, clutching the wampum belt to her chest as the nameless demon oozed out of DeLancey's body. He lacked cohesiveness, like a malleable clay figure, vaguely humanoid with no defined features.

"Right." Piper exhaled, then winced as her hands shot out. She relaxed when DeLancey froze intact.

The demon continued to emerge.

A feminine voice sounded behind them. "Is everything all right, Mr.—"

Piper whirled and froze the receptionist in the half-open doorway.

Phoebe clicked off the small tape recorder in her pocket. "Cole!"

Paige hardly dared breathe as Phoebe's plan began to unfold. Every second was crucial. One misstep and the wrong players could end up dead.

Cole shimmered in between the frozen figures of Ben and DeLancey. He taunted the nameless demon as it slipped free of the CEO and drew it away from the human host. "Well, if it isn't the demon dough boy."

Incensed, the primal evil flared into the flattened, shifting shape of a monster amoeba. In spite of having no vocal chords, the creature emitted a high-pitched sound as it threatened to engulf Cole.

Phoebe pulled a potion vial out of her pocket a second before Q'hal shimmered in. The revolting odors wafting from the vile bounty hunter rocked Paige back on her heels.

Spotting Cole, Q'hal attacked without hesitation. A crackling spear of energy shot from its raised fist.

Cole ducked.

Q'hal's lightning bolt struck the flattened primal demon. Screaming, the ever-changing form burst into flames and convulsed in agony before it was consumed in the fire.

Denied his prize, Q'hal raised his fists to launch another energy bolt.

"Phoebe?" Cole looked at her anxiously.

"Coming!" Phoebe uncorked the vial as Piper and Paige moved into place on either side of her. "Hey! Slime ball!"

Q'hal snapped his head around, spitting with fury. He fixed Phoebe with his yellow reptilian eyes. He raised his fist to fire.

The Charmed Ones began to recite. "Demon hunter on the prowl . . ."

Sensing danger, Q'hal jumped aside as Cole hurled an energy ball.

". . . concealed with no restraints," the witches intoned. "Condemned, this scourge of death so foul . . ."

Cole's energy ball missed, but it threw the smelly bounty hunter off balance.

". . . erased, its putrid taint."

Phoebe threw the vial before Q'hal could recover to fire again.

Streams of crimson smoke began to rise off the stricken demon as the caustic potion spread over his body. The mixture eroded Q'hal's garment of woven brown grass and evaporated the protective slime covering his mottled skin.

Holding a handkerchief over her nose, Paige sank to her knees. Her eyes burned from the noxious fumes roiling off the decaying demon, but she couldn't tear her gaze away.

Overcome by the hideous stench, Phoebe swooned. Cole caught her and gently lowered her to the floor. She leaned against him, her face contorted as spasms of queasiness coursed through her.

Piper held her nose with her fingers and made a circling motion with her hand, as though that would make the potion act faster.

Q'hal's death roar reverberated through the large office. It ended abruptly when his decomposed remains spontaneously combusted and vanished.

Paige cast a furtive glance around the office and slowly lowered the handkerchief. The air had been cleansed of all unnatural, odorous agents.

"You have no idea how glad I am that's over." Piper breathed in deeply and smiled.

"I think I do." Clinging to Cole for support, Phoebe got to her feet. "But we're not done yet."

The hard part was behind them, but there were several loose ends that needed tying up, Paige thought. To get the ball rolling, she orbed the wampum treaty back into the vault.

"You'd better go," Phoebe said, gently touching Cole's face. "I'll be back at the Manor soon."

"Wake me up when you get there." Cole kissed her cheek and shimmered out.

"Now let's just hope no one else misses their cues," Piper said.

They were back in position when the entire scene unfroze.

"DeLancey?" The receptionist stepped into the office, frowning.

"Uh—" The CEO, suddenly aware that the demon presence was gone, stammered in shock. His eyes narrowed with uncertainty and fear. He seemed to know that something had happened, but he didn't know what. "Yes, Ms. Olson. Go away."

The receptionist slammed the door behind her.

"We've said what we came to say, too." Piper yanked on Ben's sleeve. "Right, Mr. Waters?"

Ben faltered. "No, I'm not—"

Paige linked arms with the disoriented lawyer and flashed the CEO a smile. "See you in court, Mr. DeLancey."

"Bye!" Phoebe waved as they fled the office.

Ben regained his composure as they hustled him down the hall. His anger flared when they stepped inside the elevator. "I wasn't finished in there, Paige."

"Don't worry, Ben." Paige pressed the button for the lobby. "Everything's going to work out great."

"No, it's not," Ben insisted. "DeLancey was right. The Sinoyat don't have a case. All I had going for me was bravado and a bluff. Now, thanks to you, I've just squandered that."

"You've got more than a bluff, Ben." Grinning, Phoebe pulled the tape recorder from her pocket. "Trust me."

When the elevator doors opened, Paige saw Inspector Morris waiting by the fountain with two uniformed officers. He was right on schedule.

"We'll be in touch, Mr. Waters!" Piper gave him a thumbs-up as she and Phoebe dashed forward to meet Darryl.

Paige hung back with Ben. With miscellaneous demons vanquished, the Sinoyat problem resolved, and the rest of the day off, it was time for some fun.

"Are you busy for lunch?" Paige asked.

"Yes, I am." Ben smiled shyly and offered his arm. "Do you like Thai food? I know this great, little mom-and-pop place—"

Definitely worth cashing in a sick day, Paige thought as they strolled into the sunlight.

* * *

"Did you get it, Darryl?" Phoebe's eyes widened with anxious expectation.

Piper tensed when the police inspector hesitated. They had asked Darryl to get a search warrant for DeLancey's offices based on the information Phoebe had pieced together the day before.

Darryl drew them aside so the officers couldn't overhear and pulled a folded court order from the inside pocket of his jacket. "I got it, but I had to put my reputation on the line with Judge Stanford."

"Why?" Phoebe asked. "The tribal boundaries described in the Sinoyat's oral history are identical to the landmarks depicted on the wampum belt."

Darryl sighed. "Yeah, but—"

"But what?" Phoebe struggled to keep her voice low. "DeLancey gets the museum catalog listing the wampum belt treaty two weeks after the tribe accuses him of stealing their land, and the belt is stolen three weeks later. Didn't His Honor think the timing was just a little too convenient?"

"Given that Vista Recreation has the most to gain because the wampum treaty disappeared," Piper added. "Without it, the Sinoyat can't prove their claim."

"Suspicious but not conclusive." Darryl shifted his worried gaze between them. "Vista

Recreation's previous legal problem in Florida tipped Judge Stanford's decision in our favor, but—"

"You got the warrant," Phoebe interrupted, "so there's no problem, right?"

"That depends," Darryl said. "If this is a wild goose chase, no judge in this county will ever trust my word again."

Phoebe held up the cassette recorder. "We got DeLancey's confession on tape. That will help, won't it?"

"Not admissible in court," Darryl countered.

Piper rolled her eyes. "The stolen wampum belt is in the vault in DeLancey's office."

"You know that for a fact?" Darryl asked. "I'd really like to believe I'm not risking my reputation *and* my career busting into a CEO's private office on unsubstantiated accusations."

Piper understood Darryl's reservations. His association with the Charmed Ones had put his job on the line in the past. Still, this was an emergency.

"I swear." Piper held up her right hand. "We saw it just a few minutes ago. William DeLancey is a thief, and he belongs in prison. So go arrest him."

"Preferably *before* he has time to get rid of the wampum belt." Phoebe's eyes flashed. "No evidence, no conviction."

Darryl nodded. "Okay. We're going."

Phoebe exhaled with relief as the three cops

rushed into an elevator. "That was harder than I thought it would be."

"It's not like we make this stuff up just to complicate Darryl's professional life," Piper observed.

"Hey, Phoebe!" a man called.

Piper glanced toward the lobby entrance as a handsome man with sandy blond hair and blue eyes and a striking redheaded woman strode toward them. "Mitch and Angie?"

"Yes, and not a moment too soon." Phoebe waved and introduced Piper when the curious couple joined them.

"What's so important that it couldn't wait until after lunch?" Mitch asked, teasing.

"The scoop you've been trying to get on Vista Corporation," Phoebe explained. "We have a friend in the police department—"

"Which we'll deny if it shows up in print," Piper said. She agreed with Phoebe's decision to let the reporter expose Vista Recreation's criminal activities, but only as long as they were kept out of the story.

"Sixth floor," Phoebe continued. "William DeLancey's office. You'll figure out the rest when you get there."

Mitch was all business now. "I'll call you later."

"Me too," Angie said. "We have to get together to sort through the Sierra Sojourn pictures."

"Maybe Thursday." Phoebe waved, but her smile faded.

"Problem?" Piper asked as they headed toward the doors.

"Nothing major." Phoebe sighed. "I still have to get the pictures developed and printed. Of course, if the Sierra Sojourn land is the focus of a land dispute, the resort may never open."

They walked in silence for a moment before Phoebe dared to ask, "Have you heard from Leo?"

"As a matter of fact, I have." Piper grinned. "That's why I'm going home to whip up a privacy spell."

"What's a privacy spell?" Phoebe asked, puzzled.

"Here's a hint." Piper was still smiling, but her gaze was chillingly serious. "It probably wouldn't be a good idea to interrupt the intimate candlelight dinner I'll be enjoying with my husband tonight."

"Maybe Cole would like to catch a movie," Phoebe said.

Piper nodded. "That would certainly be less messy."

About the Author

Diana G. Gallagher lives in Florida with her husband, Marty Burke; four dogs; three cats; and a cranky parrot. Before becoming a full-time writer, she made her living in a variety of occupations, including hunter seat equitation instructor, folk musician, and fantasy artist. Best known for her hand-colored prints depicting the doglike activities of *Woof: The House Dragon*, she won a Hugo for Best Fan Artist in 1988.

Diana's first science fiction novel, *The Alien Dark*, was published in 1990. Since then she has written more than forty novels in several series for all age groups, including STAR TREK for middle-grade readers, *Sabrina the Teenage Witch*, *Charmed*, *Buffy the Vampire Slayer*, *The Secret World Of Alex Mack*, *Are You Afraid of the Dark*, and *Salem's Tails*. She is currently working on additional ideas for *Charmed* and *Sabrina*.

CHARMED
AGAIN

Piper and Phoebe Halliwell are devastated by the loss of their big sister, Prue. But even in their grief they can't forget that they, too, are in mortal danger. The power of the Charmed Ones has been broken, leaving them prey to every form of evil. Even Leo, their Whitelighter, and Cole, Phoebe's demon boyfriend, can't protect them.

In frustration and despair, Piper casts a spell to summon a lost witch and bring back her beloved Prue. The spell does work, but not as Piper intended. A lost witch is found – heir to a shocking Halliwell family secret. But can Piper and Phoebe persuade her to assume her powers and complete the Power of Three?

F E A R L E S S™

. . . a girl born without the fear gene

Seventeen-year-old Gaia Moore is not your typical high school senior. She is a black belt in karate, was doing advanced maths in junior school and, oh yes, she absolutely Does Not Care. About anything. Her mother is dead and her father, a covert anti-terrorist agent, abandoned her years ago. But before he did, he taught her self-preservation. Tom Moore knew there would be a lot of people after Gaia because of who, and what, she is. Gaia is genetically enhanced not to feel fear and her life has suddenly become dangerous. Her world is about to explode with terrorists, government spies and psychos bent on taking her apart. But Gaia does not care. She is Fearless.